The man who ate the 747

BEN SHERWOOD

The man who ate the 747

BEN SHERWOOD

PICADOR

First published 2000 by Delacorte Press,
a division of Random House, Inc., New York

First published in Great Britain 2000 by Picador
an imprint of Macmillan Publishers Ltd
25 Eccleston Place, London SW1W 9NF
Basingstoke and Oxford
Associated companies throughout the world
www.macmillan.co.uk

ISBN 0 330 48211 4

1 3 5 7 9 8 6 4 2

A CIP catalogue record for this book is available from
the British Library.

Printed and bound in Great Britain

The world records in these pages are real,
as are the places where the story unfolds.
The rest is make-believe.

dedication tk

. . . That is happiness;
to be dissolved into something complete and great.
When it comes to one, it comes as naturally as sleep.

—Willa Cather, *My Ántonia*

FOR THE RECORD . . .

This is the story of the greatest love, ever.

An outlandish claim, outrageous perhaps, but trust me. I know about these things. You see, I was Keeper of the Records for *The Book of Records*. I sifted through the extravagant claims of the tallest, the smallest, the fastest, the slowest, the oldest, the youngest, the heaviest, the lightest, and everyone in between.

I authenticated greatness.

In rain forests, deserts, mud huts and mansions, I watched men and women bounce on pogo sticks, catch grapes in their mouths, flip tiddlywinks, toss cow chips, and balance milk bottles on their heads. They demanded recognition. They insisted on a special place in history. It was my responsibility to identify the worthy.

In New York, I observed Kathy Wafler shaving the longest single unbroken apple peel in history, measuring 172 feet and 4 inches. In Sri Lanka, I timed Arulanantham Suresh Joachim balancing on one foot for 76 hours and 40 minutes. Our rules of verification are most stringent, and I made sure Mr. Joachim's free foot never rested on his standing foot and that he never used any object for support or balance. In the former Soviet republic of Georgia, I certified that Dimitry Kinkladze lifted 105 pounds 13 ounces of weights strapped to his ears for ten minutes.[1] In New York, I calculated the longest flight of a champagne cork from an untreated and unheated bottle: 177 feet 9 inches.

I snapped the photo of Robert Earl Hughes, the world's heaviest person, buried in a coffin the size of a piano case.[2]

I wrapped measuring tape around the 84-inch waists of Bill and Ben McReary of North Carolina, the world's heaviest twins. I computed the length of Shridhar Chillal's snarled fingernails, all 20 feet 2¼ inches. I recorded Donna Griffith's 978-day sneezing fit and documented Charles Osborne's hiccup attack that lasted 68 years. I spell-checked the longest word in the English language: pneumonoultramicroscopicsilicovolcanoconiosis.[3]

My specialty: all things superlative. Yet I gladly admit I

[1] Please note that Mr. Kinkladze's left ear (lifting 70 pounds 9 ounces) was considerably stronger than his right ear (35 pounds 4 ounces).
[2] Let the record show that, despite widespread belief, Mr. Hughes was not actually buried in a piano case. His coffin was merely the size of a Steinway.
[3] According to the *Oxford English Dictionary*, the 45-letter word means "a lung disease caused by the inhalation of very fine silica dust."

am a supremely average man. In size, shape, and origins, I am the statistical norm: 5 feet 9 inches, 169.6 pounds, born and raised in the Midwest. My given name, John, is unexceptional. My family name, Smith, is the closest I come to a world record. It is the most common surname in the English-speaking world: 2,382,500 people share its distinction in the United States. I go by the initials J.J., my mother's way of setting me apart from my father, John Smith, his father, John Smith, his father's father, and all the John Smiths in the world.

For all my ordinariness, I do make one claim to greatness, the kind with no official listing in The Book. Once upon a time, I witnessed the most incredible record attempt, ever. It showed me what I failed to grasp in all my years before as Keeper of the Records. I once believed the wonders of the world could be measured, calculated, and quantified. Not anymore.

In the pages that follow, I've reconstructed the remarkable proceedings, presenting the facts that I myself certified. At some point, you might wish to check on these events in The Book, but alas, you will not find any mention, not even a footnote or an asterisk. Indeed, no matter how hard you search the heartland with its corn palaces and giant balls of string, you will never come upon any statue or sign marking this singular feat. There is no official monument to this achievement, no carved inscription to read, no museum or scenic detour with a souvenir stand to make you stop and wonder: Did it really happen?

To know the truth, you must go to a town in the middle of the country where folks care about crops, family, and faith. Stay awhile, listen closely, and you will hear what sounds like tall talk about a man who ate an airplane. Yes, an airplane. Sure, it sounds preposterous, and maybe not too tasty, but drive north of town, past the windmill, over two gentle hills, and you will come upon a sloping field with rows of corn. Look beyond the red farmhouse, near the barn, and you will see a great gash in the ground.

This indentation in the earth, measuring exactly 231 feet 10 inches, is the only vestige of the endeavor. It's an unlikely spot, and an even unlikelier tale. Believe it just a little, though, and you may shed some of the armor of ambivalence that shields you from your feelings and leaves you sleepwalking through your days. You may discover greatness where you least expected. You may even decide, once and for all, to take a stand, to venture everything, like a farmer named Wally Chubb who loved a woman so much he set about eating a jumbo jet for her.

They may strain credulity, bend physics and biology, but let this place and these strange events into your life and you will know a simple truth: We chase wild dreams and long for all that eludes us, when the greatest joys are within our grasp, if we can only recognize them.

CHAPTER 2

The building on East Fourth Street was crumbling brick by brick. A homeless man was sprawled in the entryway, arms and legs splayed, a copy of *Martha Stewart Living* open across his bare chest. J.J. stepped over him carefully, saw that the elevator hadn't been fixed, and trudged up the grimy stairs to his apartment on the fifth floor.

New York, the greatest city in the world.

His apartment door was cracked open. The light from the hallway threw a fuzzy white rectangle onto the dusty parquet floor. He set his bags down and hung his jacket carefully in the hall closet. He called out, "Hello?"

The place was still a mess. A little pagoda of Empire Szechuan carry-out containers stood in one corner. He squeezed past the stove and refrigerator jammed against the wall in the entryway. When he first moved from the Midwest, the real estate broker convinced him that many Manhattan apartments had kitchen appliances in hallways, even living rooms.

The walls of the apartment were tired Benjamin Moore white, ringed at imprecise intervals with photos in spare black frames of people so familiar that they were almost family. There was Henri Pellonpää in Finland, who killed the most mosquitoes in the five-minute world championships; Alan McKay of New Zealand, who made the world's biggest soap bubble—105 feet—with a wand, dishwashing liquid, and water; and Joni Mabe of Georgia, who owned one of Elvis Presley's warts, officially the world's strangest body part keepsake.

"Mrs. Bumble!" J.J. called out. "I'm home!"

Down at the far end of the narrow living room, stooped beneath the dreary curtains, his elderly neighbor from upstairs watered sunflowers in a window box. She wore a frayed winter coat, a fedora, and headphones.

"Mrs. Bumble?"

The woman didn't waver. She continued watering. He touched her shoulder gently, and as she turned around, he could hear the tinny sound of Madonna's "Like a Virgin."

"Hello, love," she said, big red dots of rouge crinkling on her cheeks. "I wasn't expecting you back so soon. How was your trip?"

"Can't knock Paris. I brought you something." He handed her a bottle of good duty-free Chardonnay.

"Aww, thanks. I came down to get your mail and give my friends here a little drink."

Mrs. Bumble turned back to the sunflowers. They were made of plastic, coated with the black grit of the city. With a soft rag, she wiped the filth from each synthetic leaf, then sprinkled more water on them. "So? Did you meet any girls?"

"It was a business trip," J.J. said. "The records require all my concentration." Actually, he had deflected an overture from a sunny flight attendant who told him that she'd be in town on a two-day layover.

"Phooey," said Mrs. Bumble.

He knew she worried about him. He could never convince her that his brief, doomed encounters made him feel even more lonely. It had happened many times. He knew the brain chemistry of these ill-fated dates. A whiff of compatible pheromones, a neurochemical rush, giddiness, pleasure, then, as the dopamine wore off, the stark reality. She barked like a dog in her sleep or had a rap sheet as long as the Nile. Or, more often, he would disappoint her. The harder she fell for the man in the gold-crested jacket, the more disillusioned when he turned out to be just an ordinary guy named John Smith.

"There's more to love than meeting girls," he said, trying to smile. "You're looking at a man who inspires women to scale the heights of ambivalence."

"You take yourself too seriously. You sit there all day with your stopwatch and your measuring tape. You never have any fun. What about the pretty girl from Denmark with the hula hoop? I liked her."

"Not my type," he said, plunking down on a furry couch. "She wore me out."

"Okay, what about that beautiful woman, the one with the world's longest neck. Where was she from?"

"Myanmar," he said. "Remember? She spoke no English?"

"Details, details. Let's see, there's the girl in six B. She works in advertising—"

"—We bored each other to stupefaction."

"You're too picky," Mrs. Bumble said.

Her attention shifted. "You know, the catalog said these sunflowers were lifelike. But real sunflowers follow the sun across the sky." She looked up at the light sneaking between the walk-ups across the alley.

"We could get some real ones," he said.

"This place wasn't meant for flowers."

Mrs. Bumble pulled a bottle of Schlitz Malt Liquor from her coat pocket and took a swig. "Mail is on your bed. And you've got two messages on the machine."

"Thanks for keeping an eye on things," J.J. said. He went to the tiny bedroom, a square cell with an Ikea bed and nightstand. He punched the rewind button on the answering machine. Had the flight attendant tracked him from his airplane seat to his home? It had happened before.

The first message played. The voice was distant, surrounded by static. "Mr. Smith, hello, it's me, Mitros Papadapolous. I'm ready for you now. I've conquered all the obstacles. You'll see. I can do it now. Hello? Mr. Smith?

Do you hear me? Operator? Is the line still there? Come and see me in Folegandros, Mr. Smith."

"Who's he?" Mrs. Bumble asked from the doorway.

"Good guy," J.J. said. "Wants to break one of the toughest records."

"What's that?"

"Standing still."

"What kind of record is that?"

"Not easy. Trust me. The motionlessness record is 18 hours 5 minutes 50 seconds."

"Why would anyone do that?"

"A place in history," J.J. said. "A whiff of immortality." The second message began. The tape-recorded voice of his boss, Nigel Peasley, slithered through the speaker.

"It's Peasley here. I want to see you in my office Monday morning."

Thoughts of a sunny stewardess and the relief of being home vanished as J.J. wondered what evil Peasley was now about to unleash.

"You're late."

Peasley's high-pitched voice carried an impeccable British accent. He wore a chalk-striped navy suit, red braces over a crisp blue shirt with a white collar, and a university tie. Mustache geometrically groomed, fingers delicate, he had his hands clasped so he could avoid the obligatory, too-vigorous American handshake. And J.J. Smith's hand, he was certain, would be sticky or damp.

"Jet lag. I overslept," J.J. said. He dipped his head. "Sorry."

"No record in Paris."

"No, sir. No record."

Peasley examined the poor sod sweating before him. What to do with this burnout? How was he ever going to whip things into shape if his field team couldn't come up with something big, something truly spectacular? Headquarters dispatched him to grow the business in America, to improve circulation of The Book, and to expand the famous brand far and wide. But now carbonized lumps like J.J. Smith were bringing the company down.

"You've been here 14 years," Peasley said, tossing Smith's personnel file down on his expansive oak desk. It slid to the far corner of the polished surface. "You haven't landed anything since the world's biggest feet—"

"Actually, sir, you're forgetting the hair-splitting record. Alfred West of Great Britain? Split a human hair 17 times into 18 parts.—"

Peasley scrunched his nose in disdain. "That was more than a year ago. Tell me, what's wrong? You can talk to me." It was a technique from a weekend management course he endured. Put yourself on the side of your employee. Imagine wearing his shoes, even if you would never go near rubber soles.

"Nothing's wrong," J.J. said into the brutal silence. "What about the world's fastest snail? You sent me to the World Snail Racing Championships in England. Remember little Archie? Set the record on the 13-inch track in 2 minutes and 20 seconds."

Peasley glowered. "Do you watch television, Smith? Have you seen *The World's Most Amazing Videos?* Last night, a man on an American aircraft carrier was sucked into the engine of an A-6 fighter jet. He vanished right into the turbine but managed to survive. Just a few bumps and bruises and a broken collar bone."

Peasley wagged a long finger at J.J. "That's our competition. Big stunts. Crowd pleasers. When animals attack. When inmates escape. When girl scouts go bad. Do you really expect us to dominate the new millennium with the world's fastest snail?"

Contempt gurgled in Peasley's windpipe. He failed to suppress a sneer. "You think you know everything. Well, here's a little surprise for your database. The home office wants to bring me back. Downsize this branch to two field operatives with laptops. Eliminate redundancies."

"What are you saying?"

"Lumpkin and Norwack are putting you to shame. They bring in great records. They hunt for the Big One, while you . . . you split hairs and chase snails."

Peasley could smell J.J.'s discomfort. Let the little bugger suffer. His performance reviews had been stellar in the early years, according to his predecessor's file. But for too long, he had coasted. Past laurels and seniority be damned. He might know all 20,000 records by heart and remember every staff member's birthday, but from now on only results would protect him.

"Great ones don't come along every day," J.J. said. "I've got ideas, though."

Peasley looked over the tops of his reading glasses,

straightened himself in his chair. He picked lint from his sleeve. "Bring me back a record that will make the public take notice. Must I say 'or else'?"

"No, you've been clear."

J.J.'s chair scraped the floor loudly as he stood to his feet. "Anything else?"

Peasley flicked his wrist. He had already opened the next file. "Get along, then. Do whatever it takes. As you Yanks say, make it happen, and make it happen fast."

The Book was born of a bet. One weekend in the woods, two hunters debated whether the golden plover was indeed Europe's fastest game bird. With no immediate way to resolve their wager, the friends realized that a book settling the score on this and other factual matters would be a surefire best-seller around the world. Thus in 1955 The Book came to life, and over the years, it was published in 70 countries with 22 foreign-language editions.

Imagine the headquarters of The Book, and you might conjure a venerable institution, an imposing granite building, like a courthouse, with wide steps and brass handrails, and at the great front doors, a long line of people juggling bowling balls and swallowing swords, waiting for an audience with the record keepers. Inside you may well conceive a whirring place with hundreds of researchers poring over submissions from the world's 190 nations. In short, here would be a haven of miracle and wonder, where brilliant men and women with advanced degrees and eons of expertise vet and crown the world's greatest feats.

Pull back the wizard's curtain, though, and you would discover reality. American headquarters occupied an anonymous hunk of a building, consisting of a modest suite of offices, like any drab insurance agency, its walls unadorned, cubicles spare, lacking even illuminated display cases for world record memorabilia. Above the receptionist's desk, a lonely and rather swollen head of garlic languished on a shelf, the world-record holder, weighing two pounds ten ounces.

Enclosed in his work space, wedged behind a gray steel desk, foot tapping the waste basket, J.J. waited for the fear to pass. Would headquarters truly reduce the U.S. operation to a laptop office? Sacrilege! What would become of him? Fourteen years as a record verificationist prepared him for exactly nothing. There was no life beyond The Book.

He lifted his eyes to the wall across from his desk and the photo of a beaming young woman, Allison Culler, winner of the biggest Twister game of all time. Next to her stood an optimistic young man in a blue blazer with a gilded crest, surrounded by 4,160 players. How many years had it been, five? Ten? Where had the exhilaration gone, the rush of witnessing greatness, chronicling moments for all time? Whoa, those thoughts led only to a dead end. He veered sharply. Nothing gained by self-pity. A stack of submissions stood in front of him and a cold cup of coffee beside the silent telephone.

The weekend mail had already been sorted by the Review Committee, an extravagant phrase that actually described Trudy Dobbs, the shapely 23-year-old part-time secretary who answered the phones and processed submissions. Dobbs was a one-person Review Committee. She collated entries worthy of consideration and attached an official cover sheet for internal processing.

By the time the low light of afternoon arrived at the window, J.J. had evaluated nearly all of the submissions. Lumpkin and Norwack, the young hotshots, were out verifying new records. Down the hall, Peasley was surely engaged in some sly sabotage.

He flipped through the remaining pages sent in by strivers and seekers from around the world. A man in Honduras claimed he could contort his intestines to resemble Elizabeth Taylor's face. J.J. took the enclosed X ray and held it up to the light. There was no movie star in its shadows. He X'd the rejection box on the cover page.

Next, a fellow in Canada purported he could make a high-pitched noise emanate from the top of his head and shatter glass. Ludicrous. He X'd the box. Rejection.

A woman in France asserted she could gallop on her hands and knees and jump 16-inch hurdles. Merely a variation on crawling, and there were already plenty of these records in The Book. Rejection. X'd again.

A man in Pakistan proposed walking backward from Gilgit to the Mintaka Pass. The Book had plenty of walking-backward records, but who had ever heard of Mintaka? He made a note that the applicant should consider walking backward on the better-known Khyber Pass and it would be considered for a record.

A team of salt miners in Poland planned to set the record for the deepest subterranean hot-air balloon flight. Their goal was to fly the length of a cavern more than one mile underground. An excellent prospect. He marked an X:

accepted. He would look into it later, but it was hardly the kind of big record Peasley wanted.

A gentleman in Huntsville alleged he could divine water with his private parts. Out of the question. No records were allowed involving private parts.[4] This was a book for all ages. The arbiters of decency and decorum always prevailed. Another X. Rejected.

J.J. finished the general submissions and turned to another folder, the Kid's File. This was the weekly compilation of letters from youngsters across the country, The Book's most devoted readers. His very first job, entry level all those years ago, had been answering thousands of these letters. Rising through the ranks, he often returned to this file for inspiration. These scrawled notes sprang from hope not yet hardened, from dreamers who still thought everything was possible.

He knew that feeling somewhere deep inside. It touched him first at age 10. It was a hot summer day on the little square lawn behind his house, the day he collected 116 four-leafed clovers. He ran straight to his mother in the kitchen, where she helped him compose a letter to *The Book of Records*. He wrote it longhand, lovingly, and sent it off to the Review Committee. Every day after school, he waited by the mailbox, hoping for good news. At last a letter in a fancy envelope arrived, and he ripped it open to see the blunt words. The world record in this category was set by a Pennsylvania prison inmate who

[4]One small exception should be noted. The world's most valuable privates officially belong to Napoleon. Removed during his autopsy and put up for auction, the one-inch-long specimen was described in the catalogue as a "small dried up object." It was later purchased by an American urologist for $3,800.

gathered 13,382 four-leaf clovers during his recreation time in the yard. There was not even a thank you or the slightest hint of encouragement.

He knew then, shaking beside the mailbox, that he would never set a world record. After all, he was just another John Smith from Ohio, ordinary in every respect. From that searing moment, though, he found his life's ambition. He would work for *The Book of Records*. He would know and bestow greatness.

He flipped through a stack of messy letters, block printed on scraps of notebook paper.

Whoever Opens the Mail,
My cow is the oldest cow.
What is the age of the oldest cow that you know?
Look on the back of this paper. I drawed a rooster for you.

Tommy Ruskin
Fremont, Wyoming

He turned the page and inspected the crayon drawing of a turkey. Then he scanned the photocopied response that was paper-clipped to the boy's letter. He had dictated it before he left for Paris.

Dear Tommy,
Your rooster picture is great. A Rhode Island Red! I'm very impressed.
Thank you for writing about your cow. According to our records, the oldest bovine lived 48 years and nine months. Big Bertha died on December 31, 1993

in County Kerry, Ireland. By the way, the record for the heaviest cow is 5,000 pounds.

Good luck setting your own world record someday, Tommy. You're well on your way.

> Yours,
> J.J. Smith
> Keeper of the Records

The rest of the pile would have to wait for his response, but he thumbed through, loving the misspellings and funny grammar, hoping to find something, anything, worth pursuing.

Dear Mister,

I'm Hank Caldwell and my specialty is making french fry sculptures. Big ones and little ones and never with glue.

I read your book and don't see a record of french fry sculptures. Is there one?

> *Hank Caldwell*
> *Chilton, Alabama*

To the Book of Records,

This is a new record category. My 2 front teeth are the mostest spread apart. Doctor Honig measured and the distance is ⅓ inches. I can push a fish stick sideways between them.

Everyone thinks I got a tooth knocked out, which I didn't. I'm sending a picture for you to see.

> *Thanks,*
> *Jeanie Vandeveer*
> *Boone, Indiana*

Dear Mr. or Mrs.,

I have the hardest hair in the whole world! Every day before school, I spray it with hair spray so when my friends touch it it doesn't move even a little. I spray at night and it stays in the same place even sleeping. I use gel sometimes to make it more harder. Will you put me and my hardest hair in your book?

Sincerly,
Brett Kwong
Madera, CA

Dear Book of Records,

Hi it's Daryl again. This time I want to set the record for having the most sleep in my eyes. Does it count?

Send info.
Daryl Healey
Braxton, West Virginia

As he closed the file he noticed one letter had slipped onto the floor. It was written on a piece of lined, hole-punched paper.

Dear Record Man,

You won't believe it, but I know someone eating a 747, the airplane with the hump on top.

Every day he eats some, no matter how bad it tastes. I sware.

People think he's crazy, but he isn't. I know why he's eating it. He has a good reason. Believe me.

I looked in your book. You don't have this one yet.

> *The Guy Who Knows.*
> *Superior, NE*

Ps. I'll get in trouble in anyone finds out I sent this letter.

PPs. What's the record for flying the furthest on a kite?

On its face, the submission deserved an automatic rejection. For starters, anonymous submissions—*The Guy Who Knows*—turned out to be hoaxes most of the time. There were plenty of practical jokers out there, and the record keepers had to be vigilant. Furthermore, The Book had officially banned gluttony records in 1989 for a simple reason: It couldn't afford the legal exposure with all those gourmands choking on hotdogs, goldfish, light bulbs, and once even a Cadillac Seville.

Still, he reread the letter. There was something authentic about it. He searched the penciled lines for clues. *I know someone eating a 747.* It was ludicrous but delicious, absolutely too good to be true, the kind of record Peasley craved. Lumpkin and Norwack would be put in their places. Gastronomical feats had always been the most popular in The Book until the ban, and J.J. had inventoried plenty of them.[5]

---

[5] To be specific: J.J. watched Peter Dowdeswell scarf 13 raw eggs in one second; John Kenmuir eat 14 cooked eggs in 14.42 seconds; Bobby Kempf consume 3 lemons, including skin and seeds, in 15.3 seconds; and Jim Ellis down 3 pounds 1 ounce of grapes in 34.6 seconds.

The blank gray face of the computer stared at him. He slid his mouse over the pad, tapped his password on the keys. In a moment, he logged onto the Internet. There were a few easy traps to run. If a man was eating a 747 in America, no matter where, someone, somewhere must have written about it. He entered key words to form a search request, but nothing came up.

Hope faded and the bleakness of the meeting with Peasley descended over him. In the gloom, he inspected the letter again. *Superior, Nebraska.* He clicked the map finder on his computer. There were 23 towns and cities in America named *Superior,* not including two South Superiors and one North Superior. It was hardly notable. Midway held the U.S. record with 212, followed by Fairview with 202.

With a few more mouse clicks, he located Superior smack in the middle of the country, right on the border with Kansas. The town was exactly 1,499 miles from New York and 1,519 miles from Los Angeles. It called itself the Victorian Capital of Nebraska, whatever that meant. Then he found the town newspaper, *The Superior Express.* He rummaged through its archives. There were articles galore on grain prices, the Future Farmers of America, and high school football, but nothing, not a mention of a man eating a 747.

As he turned the idea around, it seemed more and more impossible. The problem really wasn't consuming an airplane. God knows, people ingested all sorts of things. In fact, J.J. verified the record for the worst compulsive swallowing. A woman with "slight abdominal pain" turned out to

30

have 2,533 objects in her stomach, including 947 bent pins.

Gobbling a grocery cart, golf clubs—no sweat. Even an airplane was feasible. The biggest obstacle would be getting your hands on a jumbo jet. It certainly didn't come cheap, and they weren't exactly giving airplanes away on the Great Plains.

An idea. He turned to a database of newspaper and magazine articles. He entered a new combination of words and waited while the computer chewed on the request. Then, a flashing light on the screen. One hit. He tapped a key and scanned the story.

SUPERIOR, NEBRASKA (AP)—(July, 1990) A 747 cargo jet crash-landed today in a corn field.

Eyewitnesses said the 747 was forced down in a lightning storm. The pilots abandoned the jet and were seen hitchhiking north on Route 14.

There were no passengers on the plane and no reported injuries. The aircraft survived the impact largely intact.

According to the Federal Aviation Administration, the plane was en route from Chicago to an aviation junkyard in Arizona.

The plane is owned by PLF Inc., an air freight company that recently filed for protection under Chapter 11 bankruptcy regulations.

Bingo. A 747 had crash-landed in a farmer's field. Abandoned there as junk. J.J. fell back into his chair. It was conceivable—albeit preposterous—that someone actually had a jet in his backyard and was trying to eat it. Perhaps the whole idea was the product of an overly active imagination, the cruel invention of a young letter writer. Or maybe, the record of all records. J.J. knew what he had to do. If it turned out to be bunk, he could certainly stir something up. Somewhere out there in Nebraska, there was a farmer with the biggest ear of corn or a schoolboy with 13 toes.

He booked the next Dollar Jet to Omaha.

CHAPTER 3

The wind hurried over the vast flatness as if it wanted to get somewhere, fast.

J.J. felt the same impatience, but kept his rented Taurus at the posted 75-mile speed limit. The drive from Omaha took three hours, a straight shot west on Interstate 80, past Lincoln, south at Exit 332 Aurora onto Route 14. It was early morning, the sun glancing off the rear-view mirror. The highway led to the middle of absolutely nowhere or the middle of absolutely everything, depending on how you looked at it.

Usually in neutral on his way to a record event, J.J. was in high gear today, like his early days with The Book. A procession of country singers drawled on the radio. *"If the phone don't ring, it's me."* At the top of his lungs, he joined the chorus. The windows were down, the air warm and dry. He liked to drive and certainly knew about roads. His father, John Smith, had worked his whole life for the Department of Transportation, 40 years as a route marker in northeast Ohio. He painted stripes on every road in District Four all the way to Lake Erie. Every marking, perfect and precise. Each line exactly 4 inches wide. Each dash precisely 10 feet long. Each imprint exactly 15/1000th of an inch thick. "Son," he liked to say, "I've learned one thing in life: Stick to the straight and narrow and stay in your own lane." His father did just that, all his life, kept to the slow lane, until a Mack truck jackknifed outside Akron and he was gone.

To honor his dad, J.J. proposed and created a whole section in The Book on roads. He measured the longest, the worst, the highest, the lowest, the widest, the steepest. He traveled to Ripatransone, Italy, to verify the narrowest: Vicolo Virilita, 1 foot 5 inches wide. He visited Bacup, England, to inspect the shortest: Elgin Street, 17 feet long.

J.J. knew the merit of his father's philosophy and he, too, stayed in his own lane. No point going too fast, no point too slow. He drove that way too as the road, a smooth two-lane affair, passed through the town of Clay Center. A sign pointed the way to the Roman L. Hruska Meat Animal Research Center. J.J. knew his American history. Roman Hruska, the late senator from Nebraska, was infamous for defending a lackluster Supreme Court nominee with the question: "What's wrong with a little mediocrity?"

What's wrong with a little mediocrity . . .

J.J. knew the answer. Here, in this utterly ordinary countryside, he hoped to find the greatest record of them all. The map on his lap indicated he was entering the Republican River Valley—hardly a valley at all, more like a little dent in the plains. Pressing forward, as the blacktop became narrower, squeezed on both sides by the fields, he had a sensation of living in a closed loop. Born in one of these interchangeable towns off the interstate, he fled Ohio as soon as he could drive. Yet no matter how far he traveled, to Marrakech, Zanzibar, and beyond, he always seemed to end up on a road to a small town, measuring the biggest watermelon or the longest clothesline.[6]

Today it was Superior, population 2,397. The sign on the outskirts of town was simple: "Nebraska—The Good Life." He drove slowly, past the tallest landmark, a blue water tower, and down streets lined with brightly painted Victorian homes, well-sprinkled green lawns, and flower beds of blooming zinnias and orange lilies. He explored the business district, four blocks of tidy storefronts. The windows were sprayed with messages: GO WILDCATS. The only sign of intrusion from the outside world was a Pizza Hut. The streets and sidewalks were empty. The white sun flattened what was already flat enough.

He pulled to a stop in front of the Hereford Inn, a red-shingled saloon on Main Street, got out of the car and stretched his legs. A neon sign in the window said: BREAK-FAST, ANYTIME. The wind streamed across his face, a warm wind, different from the sharp, quick gusts on the East

[6] For the record, the biggest watermelon weighed 262 pounds; the longest continuous clothesline measured 17,298 feet with newly washed laundry fluttering the entire length.

Coast. This was an old wind, roaming the plains, covering hundreds of miles, taking with it, speck by speck, the towns and lives along the way. The wind seemed to welcome him to Superior.

The Hereford Inn was deserted. The room was long and dark and smelled of frying pans and beer. A policeman under a big hat read the newspaper in the corner.

"Morning," said the woman at the bar. She was short, squat, and stuffed into her red and white uniform. The pin on her blouse said: MABEL.

"Can I help you?"

"Cup of coffee, please."

"Sure, anything else? Eggs? A doughnut? We make 'em fresh."

"You got glazed?"

"Uh-huh," she said. "You passing through?"

"Not sure yet." J.J. took a bite of the doughnut.

"That'll be a dollar even."

"Got a question for you," J.J. said. "You happen to know a guy around here eating an airplane?"

"Guy eating a what?" Mabel glanced over at the policeman, who looked up from his newspaper. "Why would anyone in his right mind do something like that?"

"Good question," J.J. said.

"Hey, Shrimp," Mabel called out. "You hear about anyone eating an airplane in these parts?"

The policeman sprang from the table. He was as short and skinny as a Slim Jim, his slight stick figure overwhelmed by the folds of a well-starched uniform. His gaunt face was hidden under the shadow of an enormous hat. Strapped to his slender waist, his Colt .45 automatic looked more like a cannon.

"Who's asking?" the policeman said.

"J.J. Smith. From New York City. I'm with *The Book of Records* and I'm here to—"

By the look on their faces, he knew he had their attention.

"What do you know? New York City," Mabel said.

"Welcome to Superior," the policeman said. "You just pull into town?"

"Just got here," J.J. handed over a business card.

The police chief inspected it carefully.

"'Keeper of the Records'," he read. "My wife is never gonna believe this. You know, she has the worst breath on earth. You might want to look into that."

Mabel laughed. "Speaking of records, you should see my boyfriend, Hoss. He's got the world's biggest, uh,—"

J.J. cut her off quickly. "I'm in a bit of a hurry. Can you help me find this man eating the plane?"

The police chief tightened his belt a notch.

"We can help you find anything you want," he said. "We know everyone's business around here."

"That's great. Where do I—"

"Cool your heels," the chief said. "We like to take our time here, get to know each other. I'm Chief Bushee."

"You can call him Shrimp," Mabel said. "Everyone does."

The chief put his hand on J.J.'s shoulder and led him back to the table. "Keep the coffee coming, Mabel. We're gonna visit here for a while."

J.J. slid into his chair. He wanted to blast out of the Hereford Inn, find the man eating the plane, and get started. He could hear his mother's voice as she put him to bed, reading from the story book about the unruly child named Max: "And now, let the wild rumpus start!" He wanted to start the rumpus, but he had to keep his cool.

"We've got a lot to talk about," the chief said. "You ever hear about the prison escape up in Grand Island? Guy made a 30-foot rope out of dental floss and climbed right out the window. Took him two years. Is that a world record?"

The blue blazer with the gilded crest flapped madly on its hanger in the backseat as the Taurus bumped along the two-laner heading north out of town. The road wandered past a cemetery and a few farms before dribbling into the fields. J.J. drove along looking for the old windmill.

Coffee with Shrimp had gone for more than an hour. Rapid fire, he learned about every pretty girl and every unfaithful farmer in the county. He also heard about the chief's desperate struggle to stay *above* the minimum weight requirement for Nebraska police officers. Shrimp weighed just 114 pounds. The limit was 120, and the annual physical was just weeks away.

After four doughnuts and two milkshakes, a "1018" emergency radio call interrupted their talk. A bobcat had fastened its fangs onto Mrs. Esther Hoshaw's leg. The 89-year-old woman had whacked the animal on the nose with her dandelion digger and driven it off, but now she needed medical help.

Before running off, Shrimp scribbled directions to a farm on the outskirts of town. It was the roundabout way to get there. On foot, cutting through the Mullet family's wheat fields, it only took ten minutes. But he didn't want the newcomer getting lost.

On the ridge up ahead, where the heat rippled on asphalt, J.J. saw a broken Fairbury windmill ravaged by weather, just two beaten blades still cutting the air. He turned right onto a dirt road running beside a stream. It crossed over a wooden bridge, climbed up a hill, and gave way onto sweeping land. The cornstalks were lush green. In the middle of the fields, he saw a red farmhouse and barn faded by the sun. A brown dog slept on the porch. A rooster ran across the front yard.

Then he saw it for the first time, unmistakable, unbelievable.

A 747 in a farmer's field . . .

He stopped the car by the side of the road. He wanted to remember every detail. He wanted to remember the way the sunlight glinted off the tail and rudder. He wanted to remember the exact angle of the jumbo jet jutting from the ground. He wanted to remember the way the plane stretched out against the horizon, like a giant nesting bird. He wanted to remember the sensation of awe. In all his travels, he had never ever seen anything like this.

He left his car on the road and walked through the rusty gate with its hand-painted sign: TRESPASSERS WILL BE VIO-LATED. He tramped up the dirt lane toward the farm, and as he came closer, the perspective shifted. Now the barn was dwarfed by the remaining fuselage. Up close, he could see the tail end of the plane was as solid as Boeing had built it. The marking on the fin was simple: an American flag. From the nose cone all the way past the wings, the plane was picked clean, a metal carcass under the hot sun.

J.J. felt the full blast of the discovery. A 747 was no run-of-the-mill jet. It graced the pages of The Book as the world's largest jet airliner and, perhaps, the most important aircraft ever built, revolutionizing mass transportation, hauling more than 1.6 billion passengers around the world.

The dog barked from the porch, watching every step as J.J. walked straight to the behemoth. He stood beneath the gleaming hulk of a plane and its towering horizontal and vertical stabilizers. He reached up on his tiptoes, ran his fingers over rivets and aluminum skin. Warm and smooth.

It was real, this 747, in the middle of a cornfield.

No one ever knocked. The house was always unlocked. Why was someone banging on the screen door?

Wally Chubb hauled himself off the couch, turned off the Weather Channel, and searched the living room for his orange hunting jacket. He needed something to cover his red union suit. He was a big man with square shoulders and hands like slabs of steak. His face was long and wide, covered with bristle the color of rust. He patted down his bushy hair and lumbered to the door.

"Who's there?"

A man in a blue blazer stood on the porch with his hand outstretched. He was too dressy to be a salesman, too good mannered to be a debt collector.

"Afternoon," the stranger said. "How you doing today?"

"Can't hurt a Christian," Wally wiped sleep from his eyes. "What can I do you for?"

"You Walter Chubb?"

No one ever called him Walter, except for school principals and lawmen.

"You from the IRS?" Wally asked.

"No," the man said. "I'm here about the 747."

"What 747?" Wally kneeled down to his golden retriever. "Arf? You see a 747?" The dog yelped and licked his face.

"Look here," the man said. "I've got a few questions about the plane."

"I knew it," Wally stood up. "You're a Fed. Aviation Administration, right?"

"Not even close. I'm with *The Book of Records*. Came all the way from New York. Name's J.J. Smith."

"What do you want with me?" Wally said.

"Are you eating that plane?"

Wally just stared.

"No one's ever eaten a 747 before," J.J. said. "This is the first time ever. It could be a world record."

"What do you get for setting a record?"

"A certificate and you're in The Book."

It didn't sound like much. A piece of paper and your name in a book. He wasn't eating the plane for any reward.

"Think you came a long way for nothing, mister," Wally said. "I can't help you."

"But wait—"

As Wally started to close the screen door, he saw his best friend riding up the dirt path on a bicycle. "Hey, Nate!" he called out.

Nate Schoof got off his bike and leaned it against the house. He wore square black Kissinger glasses, his hair shined with a good coating of Brylcreem, and his Wildcats T-shirt and Wranglers looked ironed.

"Interrupting something?" Nate asked.

"Fella here is looking for a man eating a 747."

"Who'd be crazy enough to do that?" Nate said.

"Beats me," Wally said.

J.J. handed Wally a business card. "Thanks for your time. I'll be at the hotel in town."

"Good visiting with you," Wally said.

J.J. rushed down the dirt road back to his car.

A man eating a 747. It transcended astonishment. Edgar Snavely at *Ripley's Believe It or Not* would have a cow when he found out. Too late! The record would be all locked up for The Book.

Wally Chubb's resistance would be easily overcome. He'd been through this dance many times. The locals were simply testing, but soon they'd come around. He would wait, mind his own business, and eventually they would beg to be in The Book.

J.J. checked the rearview mirror. It was filled with the

42

silvery creature that the farmer in the Halloween costume was eating piece by piece. The big man in his red pajamas was waving from the porch.

Why was he eating the plane? Was he nuts, suffering from some neurological disorder, a perfect case for Dr. Oliver Sacks? It didn't matter. People chased records for all sorts of reasons. They wanted their 15 minutes. They wanted to make money. They wanted to impress friends and family. They wanted spiritual fulfillment. Who was J.J. to judge? All he wanted was to authenticate the record, get out of town, and get Peasley off his back.

In the shade of the porch, Wally, Nate, and Arf watched the stranger head off down the lane.

"Wonder how that guy heard about you," Nate said.

"Who cares?" Wally said. "I've seen *The Book of Records*. Looked through it at the library once. Just a bunch of freaks."

"Perfect fit." Nate polished his trifocals with the corner of his T-shirt.

"Very funny," Wally said.

"You think I'm kiddin'."

"I'm gonna get you for that one," Wally said. He sat down on the porch glider that bucked a little under his weight. "So? Did you see Willa today?"

"She wasn't in the café this morning, and I didn't see her in town either."

"You hear anything about her lately?"

"Nope. Nothing. Just what I see in the paper."

"No big deal. I was just wondering."

"It's okay," Nate said. "Come on, let's go to work. I solved your problem."

"Oh yeah, how's that?"

"I'll show you."

The big wood doors to the barn swung open, kicking up a cloud of dust. A mouse scrambled through the hay. Streams of light dropped down through cracks in the roof, illuminating a huge metal contraption. It stood 15 feet high, like an oversize refrigerator, with wires, pulleys, cranks, and levers angling in all directions.

"Stopped by Ace Hardware on the way over," Nate said. "Ordered a new five-horsepower engine for the chipper-shredder. Think that'll do the trick."

"How much it cost you?"

"Don't worry about it. Missy slipped it to me for free."

"She's been sweet on you since the fifth grade," Wally said.

"Only 'cause I helped her with her homework."

"You helped everyone with their homework."

"Now look at me. I'm the guy who assigns the homework."

The two men put on aviation-grade ear protectors. Wally knelt next to the contraption, reached inside a panel, and yanked a rip cord. The machine sputtered, groaned, then died.

"You got enough gas in there?" Nate asked.

"How should I know? You didn't put a gauge on it."

"One small oversight in my perfect design. Go ahead, try again."

Wally pulled hard on the cord and the engine rumbled to life.

Nate pulled open the front door of the machine and inspected the gears. His hands darted between moving parts. With a wrench and a screwdriver, he pulled and jerked and finally, with a satisfied smile, he turned to Wally.

"Ready when you are."

Wally gave a thumbs-up, then marched out of the barn with his hand saw and giant tinner snips. He walked directly beneath the rear bulk cargo hold of the 747, the belly of the beast, positioned a creaky ladder, then climbed right up.

He cast an eye over the smooth metallic expanse. He had never seen a jet up close until that stormy night ten years ago. He had never flown on an airplane or even been to an airport. Still, he was proud of his accomplishment: He had eaten his way through the front of the aircraft, 41 SECTION, according to the markings on the frames and stringers, running from the nose cone through the cockpit, well past the wings, all the way to the tail.

Standing on his ladder, he examined the subassembly panels under the plane. Where to begin? He tapped the aluminum skin with the tip of his snips, then began cutting. It took ten minutes of hard work, first with the huge scissors, then with the saw, rocking back and forth to give the blade more edge. He liked the warm shavings sprinkling down on his sweaty face. He liked the smell of metal, bitter and raw. Finally, a four-by-four square dropped to the ground with a thud.

Wally climbed down and he picked up the chunk. It was just the right size.

"This oughta do," he said, holding up his prize.

"Good one," Nate said.

Wally climbed the splintered ladder in the barn, hauled the panel up with a rope and pulley. Then he walked along the beams that ran the length of the structure. He knew every inch of this place, spent his childhood playing hide-and-seek in all its darkened corners.

"Here we go."

He stared down into the huge contraption and saw the metal teeth spinning at full speed, like a giant Osterizer. He put on his safety glasses, then pushed the metal piece into the mouth of the machine.

It moaned, shook violently, and suddenly went silent. The darn thing was always temperamental.

"Dammit!" Nate shouted.

Wally kicked the metal side of the device with his boot, tugged up and down on the piece of 747. Slowly the teeth began to grind, chewing up the offering. Acrid smoke spewed from the back of the apparatus.

The grinding noise was extraordinary, like a great beast dying. The abrasive sound shot out of the barn, over the two hills, past the windmill, and reverberated across all of Superior. It was a grating sound the town knew well, a sound everyone tried to ignore.

Wally swung down from the rafters on the pulley rope and waited patiently in front of the contraption. He checked his watch, and finally he flipped a switch on the front console. The grinding stopped. He pulled off his ear protectors and opened a little door built into the front panel and pulled out a red bucket.

It was filled with a metallic, gritty substance that smelled of auto shops and junk-yards. He ran his thick hands through the hot ore. It felt good to the touch, not too thick, not too thin, just right.

He turned to Nate and said happily, "Time for lunch."

It wasn't the easiest thing in the world, watching your best friend eat an airplane. Some days you suspected he wasn't all there in the head. But then, on other days, he was the smartest, most insightful person you ever knew.

"Confucius was a corn inspector until age 16," Wally liked to say. "It's in *The Farmers' Almanac*. So, the sky's the limit."

There was the time he wrote a letter to Cheerios announcing he had invented a new and improved super-glue. The inspiration for this claim had come from his daily struggle to wash dried-out cereal dregs from his bowl. This indestructible stuff—the kind he chipped away with a hammer and chisel—was far stronger than Elmer's Glue-All or Krazy Glue. To prove his point, he ground down a box of Cheerios, mixed the powder with water, and used the paste to build Arf's doghouse without a single nail. It looked durable enough to him, but General Mills was unimpressed. The company didn't even bother to write a proper rejection letter. Instead, it sent three coupons for free cereal.

Nate sat in the kitchen watching Wally make lunch.

"Rose dropped off some more articles for you. Did you see the one about aluminum and Alzheimer's?"

"It's no big deal, just like all the others."

"Rose sure worries about you," Nate said. "I see her every day after work when I go to the library. She's always looking for stuff on airplane eating—like seriously, how much is too much? Yesterday, she found an article in the *Journal of the American Medical Association*. Something about too much iron and heart attacks."

"Yeah, but Doc says I'm iron deficient, so I don't worry," Wally said, standing over the stove, frying hamburgers.

Nate tossed the photocopies on the heap by the door. The pile of articles about the perils of ingesting metal had grown large over the years.

"Here we go," Wally said, bringing two plates to the table. "Cheeseburger, onion, heavy on the tomato for you. Cheeseburger, onion, heavy on the air brakes for me."

He picked up a bottle on the table filled with gray glop. "You sure you don't want a little squirt today? Helps make you regular."

"I'm already regular," Nate said.

Wally examined his burger. He squeezed the bottle between bun and patty, and an ashen ooze seeped over the lettuce, onion, and tomato.

"You got too much on there," Nate said with alarm.

"No way," Wally said. "I never go too far with this stuff."

He bit into the burger. His front teeth and bicuspids were as square and solid as most folk's molars. Good for grinding. He chewed, then swallowed, reached for his glass of milk with its noticeably gray foam, gulped some down. He took a Tater Tot from his plate with two pudgy fingers, dipped it in granular grayish ketchup.

"Remember what Mama used to say," Wally said. "Everything in moderation."

He chomped.

CHAPTER 4

Behind all the lavender and lace, the Victorian Inn was neither Victorian nor an Inn, just a roadside motel with romantic aspirations. J.J. asked for the largest room and wasted no time getting into the shower. All he wanted to do was get the grit off him. Just a few hours in the country and he already felt coated with topsoil. Scrubbing as well as he could, he cursed the tiny washcloth and miniature bar of soap. Who were these made for? What size human could actually use them? An infant, a five-year-old, but surely not the average man.

He combed his wet hair and mapped out the mission in his mind. Suddenly, the entire building shook. Then all was still. A few moments later the room shuddered again. It was a hazard of motor inns. Big rig trucks rattled rooms, and long ago he had gotten used to falling asleep with the rumbling of the 18-wheelers and headlights flashing through plastic curtains.

Then he heard another sound, instantly recognizable.

Boing. Boing. Boing.

It was the bugle call heralding his arrival, a sure sign that word was out. *The Book of Records* had come to town. He went to the window and peered down on the parking lot. Just what he expected.

Boing. Boing.

Dozens of kids of all ages bounced on pogo sticks, up and down, gazing at his window.

Boing . . .

"Mister!" one freckle-face said. "Check this out!"

Whatever country, whatever continent, as soon as they knew he was there, they always showed up. They wanted to be in The Book. They thought it was easy. With a jump rope or a Yo-Yo, they believed they could make history.

Boing. Boing. Boing.

He hated to smash their illusions. The blunt truth hurt. He opened the window and leaned out.

"I'm up to 234 jumps," a boy with buck teeth called out.

"You've got a long way to go," J.J. shouted back. "A man named Gary Stewart set the pogo stick record with 177,737 jumps in 24 hours."

The kids kept bouncing.

"That's 7,405 jumps an hour," J.J. yelled, "123 a

minute, more than 2 every second. All day and all night."

Almost at once, the parking lot went silent.

"There are plenty of other records you can try," J.J. said. "The Book's got 3,000."

The kids stood still for a moment, then took off down the street. They were heading straight for the public library. They always did. They would search for another record to break, then they would be back.

He unpacked his suitcase. He had brought along one week's worth of clothes, nothing too spiffy except for the blazer. He put on a T-shirt, khakis, and sneakers. He stuffed a notepad in his back pocket, locked the room behind him, and went to the front desk.

"How's your room, Mr. Smith?" the receptionist asked. "Comfortable enough? You've got 52 channels of cable in there."

"It's perfect," he said.

"How can I help you?" she asked.

"Ms.—"

"Nutting. I'm Meg Nutting. What do you need?" Her face was dainty with a small pointy nose, and her pale thin neck looked ready to snap under the weight of a giant beehive of brown hair.

J.J. said, "I'm looking for information about the man eating the 747."

"Oooh, I see," Mrs. Nutting said. "Well, Wally pretty much sticks to himself. Let's see, his best friend is Mr. Schoof at the high school. Teaches science and math. Only other person who might help is Willa Wyatt at the newspaper."

"Willa Wyatt," he repeated, making a note on his pad.

Mrs. Nutting hesitated, then whispered, "Don't be put off. That's Willa."

The first call came within minutes of the stranger's arrival at the Hereford Inn. A man in a Taurus with Omaha plates, asking questions about the 747. Then another phone call. In no time, all three lines were blinking in the newsroom.

Willa Wyatt leaned back in her chair. She knew it was bound to happen, sooner or later someone would come snooping around. The story would break, and even though newspaper ink ran in her veins, she didn't like it one bit.

She closed her eyes and pushed her fingers through her sandy blond hair, braided it quickly, tying it off with an old rubber band. She took a deep breath, savoring the smell of the presses. Some of her friends preferred the scent of flowers, others the aroma of baking, but Willa loved the smell of newsprint. She kicked her legs up on the desk, where she sat as a girl, watching her father put out *The Express*. He wrote the articles, developed the pictures, pasted up the pages, operated the presses, and delivered the papers.

It was the world made fresh once a week, brought right to people's doorsteps. A noble calling, her father used to say. Even though there were bigger dailies out there beyond Nuckolls County, they couldn't compete on what mattered most. If you got too big, he said, you lost touch with your readers.

Willa studied the picture of her father on the desk.

Behind the wire-rimmed glasses, his features were sharp. Square chin, black hair, brown eyes. He was sitting on the tailgate of a green 1967 Ford, bundles of newspapers behind him. It was the same truck she still used to run the papers around town. No point getting a new one, her father said.

A few years back her father decided it was time to retire. It was earlier than most men his age, but he wanted to take a whack at his memoirs, maybe even learn to paint, and, best of all, spend more time with his wife, Mae. It was hard, but he finally handed over the keys to the Superior Publishing Company. Now he spent most days listening to the Royals on the radio, scribbling on his legal pads, or going on country adventures with Mae. Once in a while, at dinner, he would say something about the layout or the coverage. All in all, she knew he liked what she had done with *The Express*.

She was proud of the little paper too. It was only 16 pages most weeks, sometimes down to eight if there weren't enough ads, but it had won some regional awards. She tapped the computer keyboard to scroll through the wires, scanning the international datelines. There was never really any question that she would take over for her father, but what would have happened if she'd gone to work for *The Omaha Herald* or *The St. Louis Post-Dispatch*? She would have ended up living overseas as a foreign correspondent, with an expense account, great clothes, exotic food, and worldly men. She envied the cool and stylish women on TV who covered war and famine without messing up their hair. Maybe some day . . . Then again, maybe not.

"No news is NOT good news," her father liked to say. On this day, there wasn't much to write about at all. The Grasshoppers—the Little League team she coached three nights a week—were going to the state championships, but if she wrote another column inch about their exploits, there would surely be an uprising.

The farmers were in the fields, planting soybeans and milo for the fall. The county weed superintendent had found severe infestations of musk thistle, one of six weeds officially declared "noxious" by the State of Nebraska. A perennial favorite on page one.

There was only one small scandal worth exploring. The town mortician, Burl Grimes, had just been elected chairman of the hospital board. A few old folks were grumbling it was a conflict of interest, running the hospital *and* the funeral home at the same time. "Out one door, in the other," someone had said.

Willa reached for the phone. She would ask old Burl a few tough questions, piss him off, maybe even lose his business for the paper.

So be it.

The intercom buzzed. Willa turned down the farm news coming over the radio. She heard Iola's mischievous voice: "There's a guy out here to see you."

"Who is it?" she said.

"Fella from *The Book of Records*. Wants to visit with you. Then she whispered: "He's kinda cute."

"Send him back," Willa said.

She knew the type. A stranger, just passing through. There were plenty of salesman and hucksters on the back roads, looking for an angle. They told stories of the world beyond. They promised a way out. Once, long ago, she fell for a sweet-talking man who sold leather-bound books. He knew the difference between Yeats and Keats, recited lines from *The Iliad* in Greek, had traveled to faraway places. She gave away her beating heart. Then one day Mr. Odysseus went off to deliver an order of books and never came back.

She was younger then, just back from the University of Nebraska. It took about two years to come to her senses. She was fine now, all healed, stronger than ever. That is to say, she was never going to forget.

A knock interrupted her thoughts. The stranger stood in the doorway. He was nice looking with a full head of brown hair and gentle blue eyes that benefited from their association with his blazer. She took her legs off the desktop one at a time.

"You can toss all those papers on the floor if you want a chair," she said.

He moved the pile, sat down, leaned forward, and handed her a business card.

"Sure is hot," he said.

"Air conditioning's out again." She bent down under her desk, unplugged the radio, and connected the table fan. She aimed the little blower right at the stranger. "That ought to help."

"Thanks," he said. "I'm burning up."

She noticed the sheen on his remarkably straight nose. Then she saw the gilded crest on his coat pocket. Pretty slick.

"We're a little busy today, Mr. Keeper of the Records," she said, reading from his card. "Got a paper to close, and I'm short on time. What do you need?"

She reached across the desk for her water bottle. She

could feel his eyes on her and wished her hands weren't stained with ink, that her nails were polished like women in the city. She pulled the rubber band from her braid and shook out her hair.

"I'll get to the point," he said. "I heard you might be able to help me with the man eating the plane."

"Who told you that?"

"A man never reveals his sources," he said.

"A woman never reveals her information," she said.

They both laughed. A standoff. She pulled off her dad's old red cardigan and saw him glancing down at her blue cotton dress.

"I met Wally Chubb this morning," he said, "and he wasn't very helpful. In fact, no one seems very helpful. Thought since you're with the press, maybe you'd—"

"What kind of world record is this, anyway?"

"Personal aviation. We've got a whole section on people and planes. Eating a 747 would go right next to the category we call 'plane pulling.' A few years ago, a guy named David Huxley in Australia pulled a 747—all by himself—298 feet 6 inches."

His face was alive with his statistics. She liked his voice, rich and deep, probably a baritone.

"The team record," he continued, "was set by 60 people in London who pulled a 747 a distance of 328 feet in 61 seconds."

"You think that's impressive, don't you?"

"Sure."

"No. Rattling off all those statistics."

"It's my business," he said, fiddling with the pen in his hand.

"Don't mean to be rude," she said. "But I'm not impressed. Don't think anyone around here is looking for your kind of attention."

She saw his gentle eyes sadden. Did she really have to be so harsh? This guy with a nice nose and good voice was just doing his job. Still, after Mr. Odysseus, it had become an involuntary reflex. She had to be on guard. For the town. And, yes, for herself.

"Tell me one thing," he said. "Why is Wally eating the plane?"

"Did I say anyone was eating a plane?"

"Look, Miss . . ." He blinked at her.

"Willa," she said. A peace offering.

He smiled, a fine dimple on his left cheek. "Willa, I saw what he's eaten of the plane. I know what's happening out there in that field. Seems like a pretty big story."

"Not really," she said.

"A man eating a 747 isn't news around here?"

"No, in these parts that's not news."

"Seems more important than what I read this morning in your paper about Mrs. Bodkin going to see Mrs. Toppin for coffee Sunday afternoon."

"Spare me the journalism lesson," she said, standing up from behind her desk. "I'm sure you can find the door."

He stumbled out into the sun and, for an instant thought he might fall over.

She was a vision, that Willa Wyatt, with her wild blond hair, caramel eyes, and long tanned legs. From the moment he walked through the door and saw her leaning back in the chair, he felt the surge of dopamine in his veins. The table fan only accelerated the buzz, shooting pheromones through the air between them right into his hypothalamus.

He could barely stay on target during their meeting. He needed information about Wally Chubb, but all he really wanted was to know more about this woman, this Willa, this editor of a two-bit newspaper in south-central Nebraska.

He knew it was wrong. He knew it would lead to disappointment. And yet, when he thought of this woman kicking him out of her office, the feeling inside him was clear and inescapable.

He knew then and there, in a town with only one stop light, that he was about to get hopelessly, irretrievably lost.

No doubt about it, Superior had once known glory. The streets and sidewalks were wide. Pioneers with big dreams had made them this way. J.J. loped down East Fourth Street toward the center of town. He could not have been farther from East Fourth Street in Manhattan. The air smelled of earth and crops. He could see the great twin towers of the grain elevator poking up beyond the rail yard. He passed the sturdy red brick post office. A sign said it closed at noon.

It was quaint, all right, maybe even pretty, but J.J. couldn't imagine why Willa would stick around here. Didn't she realize it was a losing proposition? This place was just a wide spot in the road. Like so many towns on the plains, all the young people would gradually move away, leaving only the old folks behind. It was death by slow strangulation, life sucked out breath by breath.

A few beatup trucks were parked in front of the Git-A-Bite Café. J.J. pushed open the screen door and walked inside. Lunchtime. The place was packed and hot, an ancient ceiling fan simply overwhelmed. A man in a plaid shirt with a baseball cap pulled down over his ears left a tip on a small table with a red-checked plastic cover. J.J. sat down. He ordered a cup of coffee from a waitress who had a pretty face gone flat with resignation.

"Special's on the board," she said, banging down the cup.

Nearby, an old woman and a middle-age man were eating. "Can we use that flyswatter over here?" the woman asked the man at the cash register.

"Go right ahead."

"Jimmy, you go, boy. Get the swatter."

"Okay, Ma."

The man stood up, shuffled over to the counter, reached for the swatter, and returned.

"Go ahead, Jimmy. Kill 'em."

The man whacked the table.

"Did you get it?"

"Yeah, Ma."

"Good boy, Jimmy. They sure come in lately. You don't even have to hold the door open."

J.J. wondered if he still had the appetite for lunch.

"Hey, stranger," a voice said. "Don't mind Jimmy and his ma. Harmless as flies."

A tall man in overalls standing over the table guffawed. "Mind if I have a chair?"

"Not at all," J.J. said.

"Name's Righty Plowden," the man said. "I farm a section or two around here."

"J.J. Smith."

Righty's handshake was strong, his palm and fingers cracked and rough. He was easily in his 60s, with a gray beard, and white creases radiating from the corners of green eyes. He wore a stained work shirt, jeans, and boots.

"Hope you're not one of those vegetative types," he said. "Not much to eat here at the Git-a-Life that isn't deep-fried or cut off a cow."

The waitress materialized, and Righty ordered a cheeseburger and fries. "What kind of cheese?" she asked. "White or yellow?"

"I'll take yellow.

"I'll have the same," J.J said.

As the waitress walked away, Righty leaned closer to J.J. and whispered, "She vacuums in the nude."

"No!" J.J. said.

"By golly she does. Or so I've been told." Righty tightened the bottle top on the ketchup. "We've got the same number of sickos and perverts that you do in the big city. We just know who they are and we keep an eye on 'em."

Righty laughed and said, "So, you're here about the plane."

"I am."

"You gonna put it in your Book?"

"If I can verify it."

"Where do you want to start?"

"For one thing, is he really eating it?"

Righty stroked his beard. "Can't say for sure. Never been out there myself."

"You know anyone who has?"

"Nah, Wally don't like people coming on his farm. We hear the grinding every day. It's been going on for years, ever since that plane came down in his field. Far as I know, he could be preparing for Armageddon. Stockpiling for when the UN takes over the world."

"You don't believe that."

Righty leaned back in his chair and picked his teeth with a matchstick. "You on an expense account?"

"I am," J.J. said.

Righty ordered another cheeseburger and milkshake.

"Wally's a good kid," he said. "Fact is, no one's sure why he's doing it. Doc thinks it's a disease called pica or something. Kids eat dirt. Wally eats a plane. Could also be a brain tumor making him do it. My wife, Sally, says it's psychological. Obsessive repulsive something or other."

Righty lowered his voice. "Churchgoing folks swear he's possessed by the devil."

"So?" J.J. said. "What's your opinion?"

Righty leaned back and stretched. "It's pretty simple, really. Wally's crazy in love. Simple as that. Always has been, always will be."

"Come on," J.J. said.

"I'm not putting you on a pound. Best I reckon, it started in fifth grade. Wally fell in love with a local girl and never stopped loving her. He's spent his whole life trying to prove it to her. Heck, he'd even give three fingers off his shooting hand to win her heart."

J.J. scrawled in his notebook. A man eating a plane for love? This record attempt was getting better and better. He could definitely sell it to headquarters and the world. He was back on track and in control. The Willa euphoria in his brain had subsided.

"No one pays much attention to Wally anymore," Righty was saying. "Nothing we can do about it. He'll be that way forever. And we just have to live with it."

Whack. The sound of the flyswatter at the next table.

"Good boy, Jimmy," the old woman said to her son. "You got another one."

The door to the café opened. A woman wearing a nurse's uniform entered first. Then came Willa, the bright sunlight catching her dress for a moment. J.J. could see all of her in silhouette, lean and muscular.

"Thought you were just passing through," she said as she walked by J.J.'s table.

"Behave!" Righty told her. "Our friend here is all right."

"Oh, sure," she said. "Meet my friend Rose. This is Mr. Smith from New York."

Rose had dark eyes with round cheeks and a smattering of freckles. Her hair, long and straight, reached the middle of her back. Her white nurse's uniform was neatly pressed, and she wore a yellow button on her lapel with a simple smiley face.

"Nice to meet you," Rose said.

"Pleasure," J.J. said.

Willa pulled on Rose's arm. "Have a nice day, Mr. Smith. And don't believe a word Righty tells you. He's a crazy old fool."

J.J. watched her walk to the back of the café and sit

down. Why didn't he ask her to join them? Why did he freeze?

"Where were we?" Righty said.

J.J. had absolutely no idea. He fumbled with his notes. "Let's see. 'Wally's eating the airplane for the love of a woman'." He took a sip of iced tea. "Must be quite a woman. Where do I find her?"

"Friend," Righty said with a grin, looking over at Willa, "you just did."

CHAPTER 5

It was supposed to be easy in a place like this—sticking to the straight and narrow. Two lanes in every direction. One coming, one going. No real choices. And yet J.J. had no idea what to do next.

He tried to focus on the 747, but Willa flashed in his mind. He knew the very thought of her would end up bringing him a world of hurt. He was there to verify the record, not to veer into Wally's lane. But he could feel the pull, the chemicals firing in his brain, the sensation in his chest.

He wanted to know her. He wanted the world record. But he wasn't sure if he could have both.

He glanced in the rearview mirror

and saw the boy on the bike. The kid had tailed him all through town, first to the mayor's office, then the bank, then the shopping district on Central. He kept a smart distance, 50 feet or so, falling back when J.J. wandered into a store, then pedaling fast to keep up when he drove to his next stop. The boy cut through alleyways and shot across green lawns to stay close.

He first noticed the kid in front of the Git-A-Bite. He was accustomed to youngsters tagging along when he visited little towns. They just wanted to kill the boredom, follow the stranger, and maybe even snag a free T-shirt or pin.

This kid, though, wasn't like the others. He just watched. When J.J. went into the drugstore, the boy stayed outside, peering through the window. He wasn't hiding; it wasn't a secret; he just didn't seem to want to interfere or to get too close.

J.J. drove along Central, checked his mirror and saw the boy cycling hard on the sidewalk. He slowed down at the stop sign, waited for the boy to catch up, then signaled a right turn. He passed the Crest movie theater and the public library, crossed Bloom Street, and pulled into the Dairy Queen. He parked in the lot, without looking back, and walked inside.

He ordered two large Blizzards from a pimply teenager at the cash register, then sat down at a Formica table. Through the window, he could see the boy, perched on his bike, waiting.

"Miss," he said to the clerk. "Would you mind taking one of those shakes out to the boy on the bike?"

"No problem." She looked out the window.

"You know his name?" J.J. asked.

"Yeah," she said. "That's Blake. What a loser."

Another girl behind the counter added: "Teacher's pet."

"You the guy from *The Book of Records?*" the first girl asked.

"That's me."

"What's the biggest shake ever?"

"Easy," he said. "England, a few years ago. A 4,333-gallon strawberry shake."

The girls giggled.

"Believe me," he said, "it wasn't nearly as good as this." He slurped.

Then one of the girls took the shake, walked out into the parking lot, and handed it to the boy on the bike.

"Thanks, mister," Blake said with a gappy grin. He leaned against the white-washed wall and sucked on the straw. His hair was all floppy and blond, and he wore a bright red Huskers T-shirt that reached his knees.

"Let me guess," J.J. said. "You're 'The Guy Who Knows.'"

"Yeah." Blake nodded. "Knew you'd come when you got my letter."

"Hard to resist," he said. "So how's your kite coming along?"

"Still building it."

"Biggest one ever was 5,952 square feet," J.J. said.

"Yeah, I know. I'm not going for that one."

"Oh yeah? What's your record going to be?"

"You'll see," Blake said.

"Sure you don't want to tell me?"

"Nah. Not ready yet."

An old tractor puttered down the street. The farmer at the wheel tipped his cap.

"So," J.J. said, "what's it take around here to get some information about Wally Chubb?"

"My science teacher is his best friend," Blake said. "Mr. Schoof helped build the magic machine in the barn."

"What magic machine?"

"The grinding machine. It's how he eats the plane. He grinds it into powder and puts it on his food."

"So you know Wally?"

"Yeah, I help him at harvesttime. He pays pretty good. None of the other kids will work on his crew. They think he's weird, but I like him."

"He wasn't very friendly when I went out to see him," J.J. said. "You think you could help me get to know him?"

"Sure thing. I'll help you if you help me." Blake slurped on the straw, finishing the shake. "You know, I wrote you for a reason."

"The kite?" J.J. asked.

"Like I said, you'll see."

The TRESPASSERS WILL BE VIOLATED sign was there for a reason. Wally didn't like people coming on his land. He didn't like distractions. He had acres to plant, the wind was blowing hard from the east and that meant rain was coming. There wasn't much time to get the seed in the ground. And now the guy from the record book was back. Why didn't he take no for an answer?

"I told you once, I'll tell you again, I'm not interested," Wally said, sitting atop his green tractor, like a toy under his huge frame. He wore Key overalls and a Pioneer baseball cap.

The record guy and young Blake stood side by side staring up at him like they'd never seen a guy on a two-banger before. He took off his hat and wiped his forehead, then he climbed out of the seat and jumped to the ground. He stood just a few feet from J.J. and stared down into his eyes.

"Listen to me. I don't want your record."

"Come on," Blake said. "It would be so cool."

"Cool? You know I don't care about that, and neither should you."

"Look," J.J. said, "all I'm asking is that you let me verify what you're doing so it can go into The Book. I need to see how you eat the plane. I need to photograph the process. I need to be here when you finish the last bite so it can be official."

"You need a hearing aid," Wally said. "I'm really not interested." He glowered at Blake. "I don't know why you brought him back here! You're smarter than that."

"Come on, Wally," Blake said. "If you get the record, you'll be famous!"

Wally climbed back up onto the tractor. "Both of you! Get off my land."

"Okay," J.J. said, "I'm leaving." He paused. "One last thought. A world record sure would impress Willa."

"Yeah," Blake said. "All the girls would be impressed!"

Wally scrunched his massive forehead. "Who said anything about Willa? Don't bring her into this."

"If you want her attention, break a world record," J.J. said.

"I don't want to break a world record."

"But you'll be a hero," J.J. said. "You'll put Superior on the map. People will come here from around the world. You'll be on television. In magazines."

"You got the wrong guy. I've got everything I need right here." He put one hand on the steering wheel and the other on the throttle. "Go watch Blake fly his giant kite. I've got seed to drop—"

"Wait," J.J. said. "Have you ever heard of Michel Lotito?"

"Who?"

"Michel Lotito. He's a friend of mine. The world's greatest omnivore."

"What's that?" Blake said.

"We call him Monsieur Mange-tout. Means Mr. Eat Everything in French. He's from a village near Grenoble and he's swallowed metal and glass for forty years. Eats a few pounds every day. I've watched him munch 18 bikes, 15 grocery carts, 7 TV sets, 6 chandeliers, 2 beds, a pair of skis, a bronze coffin, a computer—"

"Cool," said Blake.

"Ain't got nothing to do with me," Wally said.

"Actually, it does," J.J. said. "I verified Michel's greatest accomplishment. In Caracas, I saw him eat a Cessna 150. That's a four-seat private plane."

"So what?" Wally shrugged. A Cessna hardly compared to a 747.

"He's a friend of mine," J.J. continued, "and Michel has gotten all sorts of female attention because of his world record. Believe me, it's amazing how many women adore him. In fact, he met his wife, Marcelle, by eating all that metal. If you let me put you in The Book, trust me, you'll get everything you ever wanted."

"I'll think about it," Wally said. He wondered what would Willa say? He had never even spoken with her about the 747. Whenever they met in town, she avoided the subject. She had never written a single word about the plane. A world record and all the attention might make her madder than hops, and that was the last thing he could afford to do.

Still, maybe this Eats Everything guy had the right idea. Maybe it was worth the gamble. He leaned over the steering wheel and said, "Listen, the only opinion that counts is Willa's. If she says no, forget about it. If she says okay, then I'll go for the record."

CHAPTER 6

The lights on the softball field glowed yellow in the early-evening haze. Boys and girls in uniforms ran to their positions for the last inning of the championship game. The score was tied, but the crowded bleachers buzzed mostly with talk about the man from *The Book of Records*.

Willa sat in the stands, listening to the hubbub. Mrs. Orville Clappenfoos, secretary of the Nuckolls County Historical Society, was absolutely sure this would be the first world record, ever, for a Superior citizen. Donald Quoogie, the State Farm agent in town, worried that Wally was definitely violating some Food and Drug Administration regulation and would end up in jail.

Making notes on her box score, Willa tried to follow the softball game. She didn't want to get swept up in the 747 hoopla. A world-record attempt would end badly for the town. She knew it on pure instinct. The guy from *The Book of Records* probably wasn't a bad guy, deep down. In fact, he seemed sweet and smart. But if the world came to town, and expectations were raised, what would happen if the dream went bust? If it glimpsed a bit of hope, how would Superior ever go back to wasting away?

A ball sailed into the gap in the outfield for an extra base hit. The crowd cheered. As a girl, Willa played short-stop on this very diamond. With her good strong arm, she threw out plenty of boys, and loved it when her father recorded her triumphs in the paper. She played every sport, even flag football, and it showed in her articles. She knew the inside moves and readers loved it.

She checked her watch. Not much time to get across town for the last story of the day. The auction would begin at six. She motioned to one of the team managers, a skinny teenager with an earring and buzz cut.

"Virgil," she said, "do me a favor. Give me a holler later with the box score from the last inning."

"You bet."

"And one more thing. Tell Missy to follow through with her fast pitch. She's pulling up too soon."

"Will do," Virgil said.

She took off for her truck and drove as fast as she could across town. The sun was still lancing rays across the land when she pulled up to the Stack homestead.

Forty farmers had come to bid. They moved around silently, inspecting the farm implements arranged methodically in the yard. The Stack family had farmed this patch of land on the Republican River for 100 years, but now crop prices had collapsed, and the bank had no choice but to sell it all.

Willa had covered too many of these foreclosures in the last year, farmers saying good-bye to beloved tractors and combines, their precious acres sold off to conglomerates in Chicago and St. Louis. She had written too many words about her own friends and their families giving up after so much struggle. Week after week, her front page featured little else but the decline and fall of their way of life.

She walked to a high spot under a maple tree and watched the auctioneer. He was a circuit rider, a traveling man who had made quite a living in Iowa, Kansas, and Nebraska. He was a quick talker who seemed to think that if he did the dirty work fast, it wouldn't hurt as much. Not far from the auctioneer, Bud and Gena Stack watched quietly, their faces drawn.

The bidding started with a hush. The first sale went fast. Bud averted his eyes as his beloved tractor was sold to a neighbor for $750. Gena cried into her apron.

Willa could see that as usual there weren't many buyers, just a lot of lookers. It was strange how so many farmers came to watch. It was like the traffic jams on the interstate when a car went off the road. Folks wanted to see the wreckage. There but for the grace of God . . .

Willa was taking notes when Tom Fritts approached in a white Stetson, matching starched shirt, and boots from the hide of some uncertain but exotic creature. The town banker, he was the richest man in the county, the one who foreclosed on the Stacks. He was an old friend of her father's. They'd both gone to school with Bud.

"How you doing?" he said to Willa, tipping his hat.

"Better than you are, I'm sure."

"You know I hate this."

"How many more you expecting in the next few months?"

"You asking me for an article? Or you just asking?"

She closed her notepad and put her pen in her pocket.

"Four more this month," he said. "Lord knows I tried to help. But it's no use."

He shoved his hands in his Wrangler pockets.

"You see that fellow from New York?" he asked. "The man from *The Book of Records*?"

"What's that got to do with—"

"We spoke today about Wally and his plane. Tell you the truth, he makes good sense."

"You didn't fall for that, Tom? That man's a hustler. You can see it—"

"Think about it for a second," he interrupted. "We don't have much here anymore. Cheese plant's gone. Cement factory shut down. Every town has something special. Red Cloud's got the Willa Cather Museum. Omaha has the largest ball of stamps. Minden has the Pioneer Village. Cawker City has the giant ball of twine. But we've got nothing."

"Not true," she said. "We've got 124 years of—"

"That's all history. We need help now. We need a future. A world record would put us on the map. I'm not saying it would stop the foreclosures or raise the grain prices. But—"

"Can't believe it," Willa said. "You bought it hook, line, and sinker." That J.J. Smith was good, all right. He'd won over the most powerful man in town. With Tom Fritts on your side, you could do just about anything you wanted.

"Think about your dad," Tom said. "What would he say? When he bought the paper, Superior was growing. We had five railroads coming through town. We had two hotels and Main Street was hopping. *The Express* was thick as my thumb. But now look at it. You barely sell enough ads to fill your pages."

The auctioneer's gavel hit the wood box. Bud Stack's precious livestock, sold for a pittance.

"Think about it," Tom said as he walked away. "It would be good for all of us."

The night was perfect for the hunt. The air was warm and damp. Locusts whistled in the trees. The moon nudged through the clouds and cast soft light on Lovewell Lake.

Armed and ready, Wally and Nate marched along the familiar trail winding through darkened woods.

"Perfect night," Nate said.

"Couldn't be better," Wally said.

He reached into the pack slung over one shoulder and rubbed his forefinger over the lid of the Hellmann's mayonnaise jar. It was banged up pretty good, a bit rusty, but the holes on top still poked through. The old jar always came along. First, as boys, when the hunt was just a hobby. Then, as teens, when at a penny apiece, $7.50 an ounce, the catch paid for secret beer. And later, when it got serious and Nate started teaching science at school.

Wally loved these nights by the lake. There was nothing so soothing, so relaxing. But tonight his head felt heavy with indecision. What would he do about the world record? His phone must have rung 10 times that day. Folks calling to say he was going to save the town. That his parents would be proud.

They stood in a clearing on the banks of the lake. The water lapped. Wally bent over, mopped his great forehead on his T-shirt, and checked his Timex.

"I figure it's 81 degrees," Wally said.

"How's that?"

"My new temperature equation," Wally explained. "Count how many times a cricket chirps in 14 seconds and add 40."

"Last week you added 20."

"That was my old equation."

The two laughed.

"You want to flash or catch?" Nate said.

"Up to you."

"All right, you flash." Nate handed over a jury-rigged fishing pole with a battery strapped to the spinning reel and a tiny light bulb wired to the tip. "It's almost time. Any second now."

"I'm ready," Wally said. Ready for what, really? Would he ever capture Willa's heart? Or would he spend his life chasing her shadow?

Then he saw the first flicker of a light in the darkness. Then another. Almost at once, the night air glittered with fireflies.

"Show time," Nate said.

Wally waved the tricked up fishing rod in the darkness, pushed the little button on the battery pack to flash the bulb in quick bursts, a twinkling secret code. The strobing device mimicked the firefly mating ritual, males trying to impress females, a come-on in shimmering light.

He hadn't done very well in school—C+ in biology—but over the years he had learned his share about fireflies. They were beetles, really, their flicker an enzymatic reaction. Nate's word for the fireflies' glow was *bioluminescence*, a fancy way of saying the release of light from a living thing. And that was Willa for him—radiant, glowing mysteriously from deep inside. A poem about fireflies described it perfectly. Willa was "living light." A beacon.

"You just going to stand there?" Nate asked, sitting down in the grass. He unscrewed the Hellmann's jar and emptied the net. "Only got 50 critters so far, and I need a few hundred for summer school tomorrow."

"Sorry," Wally said.

Nate shined his flashlight on the beetles: red heads, black backs, yellow tails.

"You're going too slow," he said. "You gotta flash faster. Average male firefly sends 3.3 per second. Run the bulb at 4 per second, and the females go absolutely wild. Less than 2.8 per second, and they ignore you."

That was Wally's problem, entirely. His whole life, he had flashed too slowly.

As a boy, he wrote her name in crop circles in the wheat fields. Made a fool of himself, misspelling her name. The next year, he hired Ace Klinker's spray plane to

tow a banner over the homecoming game. It said I LOVE
YOU! But Willa didn't guess it was for her, and he was too
scared to tell. A few years later, and maybe a bit more desperate, he even pierced his shoulder with a hunting arrow,
went to the emergency room, and said Cupid shot him.
Again, no notice. Just crazy old Wally.

"Go on," Nate was saying. "Faster!" He scurried around
with his net, swinging forehands and backhands, swooping
up fireflies.

Flash faster.

Wally squeezed the button on the fishing rod, the light
blinked, and the air around him lit up with answers. To
lure her, he knew he had to go for the world record. There
was no greater flash, no finer way to signal his love.

Jughead's was crowded with farmers in from the fields,
shirts stained with sweat, dirt under their nails. They came
in groups, crews of workers, stopping off for a quick one
before heading home for a shower and supper. The men
huddled over small tables, drinking red beer and chowing
down wedges of pizza smothered with sauerkraut. The TV
overhead was a blur of football players in training.

J.J. sat at the long empty counter, alone. The glam-
orous life of the Keeper of the Records. He had his rules.
First and foremost, no excessive fraternizing with the
locals. It made it easier to move on. It kept life simple and
straightforward.

Another town, another bar, another night on his own.

On the bright side, at least there was someplace left on the planet where you could buy beer for fifty cents. It came in a frosted mug. It was remarkable, almost worth living in the middle of Nebraska.

"Get you another one?" the bartender asked. She had an unusually long face, heavy mascara, and curly brown hair.

"Sure, one more." Any more than that and he'd forget why he was here. He put another dollar on the counter and turned around. Loud guffaws were coming from the farmers playing keno in the next room.

Then something caught his eye. Willa came through the door. She had changed into a pair of snug jeans, a white tank top, and cowboy boots. Unruly blond hair fanned out from her head like some kind of riotous halo. She wasn't a classic beauty. Her nose was a fraction of a degree off to one side, her lips were a bit full, and her hips were a touch wide. Still, it all added up to a stunning combination, the kind that made him wobble on his bar stool.

He was all set for another brushoff, but, instead, she walked right up to him.

"Folks at the Motel told me you'd be here," she said.

"Glad to see you." Why was he so clumsy around attractive women? Just once he'd like to be suave. He tried again: "Can I buy you a beer?"

"Sure. Never turn down a free beer." She slid onto the stool beside him. "Dacy, A frosty, please."

She turned her honey eyes toward him. "Listen," she said, "I was a little rough on you before."

"That's okay."

"No. I—let's just say, I didn't give you a fair chance. I apologize."

She turned straight ahead and sipped her beer. The light caught her eyelashes, the longest he had ever seen. A world record, maybe? Shoot, what did she just say?

"Apology accepted," he said.

"You find what you want today?" she asked.

"Not really. I spoke with Wally. He's ready to go for the world record."

"I don't believe that."

"He'll do it. He just doesn't want you to disapprove. You know, I don't have any tricks up my sleeve. I mean it. Getting into The Book would be the greatest thing ever to happen to Superior."

She spun toward him, banging knees. "We don't need your brand of greatness. We're just fine the way we are."

Who was she trying to fool? She knew perfectly well the town was dying. He tried again.

"What Superior makes of this is your business. All I want to do is verify the record, and I'll be gone." He was surprised at how detached his voice sounded. Did he mean it? Could he simply verify and vanish?

"It's not my decision," she said. "If Wally wants to go for the record, it's up to him. I won't approve or disapprove. But I'm telling you, don't promise what you can't deliver."

"Trust me, I've been doing this for—"

"Trust you?" She laughed. "Not as far I can throw you."

"Sounds fun," he said. "We don't have a record for flinging humans yet." She didn't even blink. Not a crinkle of a smile. Nothing was working. Nothing at all. In just one day he had converted the whole town, except the one person who mattered.

She took a drink of her beer, closed her eyes, and threw her long neck back to finish it off. It was mesmerizing. Her throat, the muscles in her shoulders, the hair tumbling everywhere. Then she set the empty glass down hard.

"Just remember," she said. "I'm watching you. Don't you dare go hurting this town."

J.J. clutched the telephone receiver with both hands, trying to contain his glee. All systems go. He had landed the 747.

"So, we're on?" he said to Wally. "That's excellent. Excellent, indeed. Get a good night's sleep. I'll meet you first thing in the morning at the farm."

J.J. hung up the phone before Wally could change his mind, then fell back against the mushy pillows on the motel bed. He felt elated, powerful, as if he could bend steel. He looked around. The porch swing hanging in one corner of the room was charming. Even the tea-rose wallpaper pleased him. The bed was adequate, if a bit spongy. He even liked the clumsy oil painting of a cottage garden over the TV set.

He snatched up the telephone again, checked his Palm Pilot, and dialed a number he had never called before.

"Sir?" he said when his boss picked up the phone, "I wanted you to know right away. I've got a big one. A really big one."

"It's midnight," Peasley said, his clipped accent almost hissing. "Can't this wait until morning?"

"Man eats plane," J.J. said.

"Man-eating what?!"

"I've got just what you want. It's unbelievable."

"What is it then? Speak clearly."

"A man is eating a 747 because he loves a woman."

There was a long silence on the other end of the line.

"Bloody hell." Peasley's voice almost squealed. "A 747?"

"Trust me," J.J. said.

"I don't know about this. It's not an existing category and you know we banned gluttony records."

"This isn't gluttony. It's passion. The world has never seen anything like it."

"If it can be done, it would be extraordinary."

"It's a cinch," J.J. said. He was panting. His heart was thudding. Peasley had to say yes. "The man is eating his way through this airliner like it's chocolate pudding. He's obsessed and unstoppable."

"Good show," Peasley said. "I'll raise it with headquarters in the morning."

"Thank you, sir. I'll stay in touch."

J.J. put down the phone and exhaled. He could hear the pogo sticks bouncing in the parking lot. The kids were back, but that was fine. Let them boing all night long. It was celebration time.

He wanted room service. Shrimp cocktail, filet mignon, red wine. Damn his puny per diem. He earned jumbo shrimp today. He went to the desk beside the window, opened the welcome book.

Alas, no luck. No room service, so he called the front desk.

"Where's the best restaurant in town?" he asked.

"It's eleven o'clock!" Mrs. Nutting said. "Everything's closed. But the Gas 'N Shop is open all night. They've got everything."

"Perfect." It would have to do. Cherry Coke, Cheez Whiz, Funyuns, and a giant bag of Nutter Butters. A balanced meal. Yes indeed, it was celebration time.

But first, one urgent task. He checked his Palm Pilot again and found the number. It would take only one call to an old friend on the national assignment desk at the Associated Press. The story would move overnight on the national news wires, and within twelve hours Superior would become the center of the universe.

Wally watched the moonbeams caress his fields. The corn poked through the soil like the stubble of a beard, casting thousands of little slanted shadows against the furrows. He loved the first sight of new corn. His family had stirred dirt on this land for one hundred years. His great-grandfather had settled the homestead, put up the farm, planted the trees, and broke in the ground. God had given the Chubbs everything they prayed for, and then some. Once, when a frost killed all the crops, his father swore that so long as they didn't take his family or his faith, he would get through just fine.

Wally rocked in the glider, alone on the porch where he

grew up, where everyone came when his parents passed on. He had lost his family, and if they took his crops, what would he have left? Just his faith.

Arf padded over and pushed his muzzle in Wally's lap. Well, he'd have his dog, too. The mutt had followed him home from town one day. When Wally asked, "What's your name?" the dog said, "Arf." And that's exactly what he called him.

"Want your chow?" he asked. "Come on, little buddy."

The kitchen was a mess. Remains of last night's dinner—some macaroni and a few cargo door hinges—lay congealed in a pot on the stove. The garbage waiting to be burned sent up a mean smell. He scooped Alpo into a bowl and set it out with fresh water. He picked through the pile of fliers on the kitchen counter and put the newspaper on top.

He flipped open *The Express* and saw her byline on page one. Willa Wyatt. His Willa. Why wouldn't she pay any attention? God knows he had tried everything, and now, even with his eating a 747, she still hadn't called to say boo. He did this every week. Looked at the paper, saw her name, hoped she would give him a sign that she noticed his giant tribute, the greatest thing he could do to prove the size and scale of his love.

It was crazy, sure, but it was love. He made no secret of why he was doing this. Everybody else knew. Why wouldn't Willa just say a little something?

He fell for her on his tenth birthday. His parents threw a party for him in City Park right in the center of town. It was a pretty place, with a row of American elm and locust trees, a Civil War memorial, a little bandshell for summer concerts, two big seesaws, and a swimming pool with a good slide. He invited all 12 of his classmates, and his mom made a chocolate fudge cake and Rice Krispies treats. They had root beer by the bottle, and Otto Hornbussel, a retired circus clown, showed up in a red wig, baggy pants, and holding a stash of skinny balloons for twisting. The four of them spread out the paper cups and plates at the picnic table under the great pin oak with its fiery fall leaves. The celebration was supposed to start at four.

Wally watched as the cars drove by on Bloom. Davey Beenblossom was in the far back of a red station wagon and stuck his tongue out as he drove past. Missy Kringle didn't even look up from the front seat of her father's black Buick. By four thirty, his great and deepening fear was true.

No one was coming to his birthday party.

These days, folks in town liked to ask if eating engines and ailerons hurt his innards. All he knew was that nothing could hurt him as much as his tenth birthday and the proof that besides his family, no one in the world liked him. He knew he was different—bigger than the other kids, clumsier, louder, and slower in school. His parents told him to pay no never mind if he didn't fit in. "It's great to be great," his father liked to say, quoting Will Rogers. "But it's greater to be human."

Still, being human hurt every day.

That afternoon in City Park was the last time he cried. It was a hell of a cry. He buried his head in his mother's lap and sobbed for half an hour. Over the sound of his wailing, he could hear his dad cussing and stomping Otto's balloons out of pure fury.

Then he heard his mother say, "Wally, someone's here to see you."

He picked his head up, saw a green Ford truck stop in one of the parking spots. A little girl hopped out in a blue dress with a big bow in back and a matching bow in her hair. It was Willa Wyatt, a sandy blond ten-year-old who looked like a princess.

"Happy birthday, Wally," she said. "Sorry I'm so late. Dad had to deliver the papers." She gave him a present in flowery wrapping paper. It was a brand-new book called *The Wonders of the World.* He read it until the covers fell off. He saved all the pieces. They were in a shoe box under the night table next to the bed, right now.

Wally pulled the Cheerios from the cupboard. He poked the contents with a big forefinger to see if there were any weevils inside, then he poured himself a bowl. He just didn't feel like cooking tonight. He added sludgy gray milk from the fridge and brought the bowl to the kitchen table. He sprinkled some stabilizer jackscrew on his cereal, stirred it all up with his wooden spoon. He took a bite and chewed.

As he ate, Wally ran his finger tenderly over newsprint and Willa's byline. Even her name was a sign they were meant to be together. Willa and Wally. Just two letters different. How many times in school had he carved both names into the desk?

Now maybe things were turning around and soon everyone in town would be pulling for him. He was going for a world record! Willa would come. She would write about him. Maybe then she would put him on the front page. Maybe then she would realize how much he loved her. Maybe then she would love him, too.

Wally got up and let Arf go outside. He stood in the doorway staring out at the remains of the airplane, twinkling in the moonlight.

That plane was part of him now. It was going to give him wings.

CHAPTER 7

The invasion took less than 12 hours.

Shrimp watched the cavalry rolling into town. So far he had counted a dozen television trucks and 22 out-of-state license plates. It was only 10 in the morning and Superior had never been so busy, even compared to the Lady Vestey Memorial Day parade with hundreds of visitors showed up from neighboring counties.

This was different. These people were outsiders. They didn't belong here. The civic peace could easily get out of control. It was his sworn duty to make sure it didn't.

The first call had come from Edna Nippert at 7 A.M. She had seen three

Asian men at the Country Store. They stocked up on canned goods and Gatorade. What in tarnation was going on? Edna demanded to know. Then a half hour later, more strangers were spotted at the Napa auto parts store. They spoke no English and, using a phrase book, asked if there was a hotel in town. Someone thought they were probably Italian.

Shrimp had declared it an official 1089—an emergency traffic situation—and ordered the entire police department, all three officers, to get out on the roads. By 9 A.M., the Victorian Inn was all booked up. The Git-A-Bite Café had run out of Wonder Bread for toast. There wasn't a copy of *The Express* to be found in town.

Shrimp guessed that since its founding in 1875, no one had ever paid this much attention to Superior, even when a very young Lawrence Welk played at the Civic Auditorium. A few years back, *Hard Copy* had come to town for a story about Crazy Tad Wockenfuss. Drunker than $700, he had tried to kill his mother by firing two shotgun blasts from his downstairs living room chair, right through the ceiling, at her bed upstairs. He missed. Mrs. Wockenfuss couldn't bring herself to press charges against her only son, so she bought him a trailer on the far side of town. Shrimp had made a brief TV appearance, describing the hole in the ceiling and the shredded mattress.

As a lawman, Shrimp knew Superior's only other modest claim to notoriety was the fact that outlaw Jesse James and his brother Frank had a sister who lived in town. According to legend, the two spent a night once and left behind a $20 gold piece.

Now the world appeared to be on its way to Superior,

and judging from the traffic, it was heading straight for Wally's field. Shrimp reached into his lunch pail and pulled out his Thermos. With all this pressure, he knew he better not forget to eat. On doctor's orders, at least three high-calorie, high-protein shakes a day, if he wanted to make it over the 120 pound mark by the weigh-in.

On the crest of the hill, a half mile away, he saw two helicopters flying low, fast and right toward him. Clutching the Thermos, he got out of the car and stood in the road watching the choppers come closer. He shook a fist at them. They weren't allowed to fly so low. There were community noise standards. The citizens wouldn't stand for it.

As the helicopters thumped, he felt the first pang of panic. The rotor blast posed a serious threat. Twice before he'd been knocked flat by the hospital chopper from Lincoln. It was a peril of weighing 114 pounds.

He braced himself and blew his whistle frantically. They buzzed right over him. The gust from the rotors hit him hard and he staggered to stay upright. His hat went flying off his head, down the road and into the ditch. Shrimp reached into the car for his radio.

"All units, I don't know what the code is for this, but I've got two helicopters speeding on Main Street. Stop them, boys. Stop them right now."

Then he stomped his boots in the dirt and skidded down the embankment to fetch his hat. The slope was steep and wet from the morning dew. His hat, brand new all the way from Hastings, was covered with mud. He wiped it off on his sleeve and started to climb. Halfway up the slope, he saw the convoy of six big satellite trucks thundering toward him. He froze.

As they roared by, the blast of wind hit him like a twister and he felt himself sailing—arms and legs akimbo—through the air and right back into that muddy ditch.

From his bedroom window, Wally looked down on his field where several hundred reporters and photographers milled around waiting for the official kickoff of the world record attempt. The Mullet sisters from down the road were selling lemonade and cookies to the strangers. Darting through the mob, young Blake was raking in coins with his very own "Official 747 Program," created and photocopied at the public library.

Wally didn't recognize all of the people, but there were many familiar faces. Tom Fritts, the banker who loaned him money, and Doc Noojin, the veterinarian, were visiting with the mayor and the county attorney. He couldn't believe they were all there, the town's finest, spiffy in their Sunday best.

Wally examined his brand new-overalls, right from Country General, all crisp and blue. His good white shirt was starched and ironed thanks to Rose, who had stopped by earlier on her way to the hospital. She had helped him pick out his clothes for the big event, told him he looked as handsome as a prince, and planted a mushier than normal kiss on his cheek before leaving.

"Will you help me with my tie?" Wally asked.

"Sure," J.J. said. "Now remember, if you feel nervous, you don't have to say a thing. Just smile and eat the plane.

They'll shout a lot of questions. But you don't have to answer."

"You think Willa's here?"

"Definitely. I saw her on the way here."

"She sure is pretty, isn't she?" Wally said.

"Yes, beautiful."

"Prettiest girl in the world. You got a record for that?"

"Nope, too subjective," J.J. said, "but I've done some research in this area. I know a thing or two. Turns out symmetrical features are the key to human attraction. Men with well-proportioned facial bone structure have sex four years earlier on average than asymmetrical men."

Wally looked in the mirror. Big fuzzy cheeks, untamed eyebrows, and reddish brown eyes his mother once said were the color of clay from the bottom of the river. There certainly wasn't anything symmetrical about his face. Maybe that explained everything.

J.J. nudged his way in front of the mirror and examined himself.

"I'm nothing special to look at," he said, "but I do have a perfectly symmetrical nose." He ran his finger down the two-inch pathway. "No dips or bumps, the spread exactly two-thirds the distance between my eyes. The slope of the dorsum from bridge to tip exactly 45 degrees—"

He turned away from the mirror.

"Sorry to get carried away," he said. "Anyway, facial symmetry means no genetic mutations. Of course, men also want women's waists to be 60 to 80 percent the size of their hips. The hourglass figure is a biological indicator of health and fertility."

He put his hand on Wally's massive shoulder.

"You see, Wally," he said, "beauty is about attraction, and attraction is about survival."

Wally felt as if he had been whacked by a windmill. "Come on. What about feelings? What about true love?"

"Love?" J.J. said. "I hate to break it to you, but it's all brain chemistry. You see a pretty girl and you get a rush of a neurotransmitter called dopamine. That's why you feel excited. Same with happiness. It's just an electrical impulse from your left prefrontal cortex."

Wally had no doubt that his left prefrontal cortex was spinning, but he was also sure that the impulse came straight from his heart. The man from *The Book of Records* knew his science, but he didn't know beans about love.

J.J. straightened his jacket, smoothed his hair, squinted into the lights. In 14 years with The Book, he had never seen so many reporters. He faced a wall of cameras. Red lights on. Ready to roll. Beyond them he could see the white masts of the satellite trucks.

No doubt back at headquarters, Peasley, Lumpkin and Norwack had gathered in the airless conference room to watch, while in at the home office, the Lords of The Book had surely tuned in to monitor the announcement.

"Ladies and gentleman," he began, "I'm pleased to welcome you—"

He saw Willa in the front row, surrounded by journalists from the big and little city papers and TV stations all over the world. She wore dark sunglasses, her long legs were crossed, and she wiggled one foot in a little circle. God, she was beautiful.

If only he could impress her . . .

Unmistakably, she frowned at him, scrunching her nose and shaking her head, and it was enough to make him fumble with the pages of his remarks.

He felt perspiration on his back, a trickle between his shoulders, and he took the quick way out. "We're here today to begin the official certification of Wally Chubb's attempt to eat this Boeing 747."

"How dangerous is this record—" a journalist shouted.

"We'll take questions in a moment," J.J. said, "but with no further ado, I present Mr. Wally Chubb."

The pasture was full of folks Wally had known all his life, the people who barely raised a finger from the steering wheel to greet him when their trucks passed on the road. Now they wanted to be part of what he was doing. His father had told him someday people would finally understand him, appreciate his gifts, and recognize why he was special.

It had been a long time coming.

It all began, really, the night the plane dropped from the sky. He was sitting on the porch at dusk with a glass of milk watching one of God's great light shows. The sky was nearly black with thunderclouds. Lightning sliced the sky every few seconds. The rain came next, in torrents, drowning the fields. Arf's doghouse—lovingly glued together—disintegrated in the downpour.

Then, a flash illuminated a shiny speck across the

cornfield. In the next bolt, the fleck was bigger. It looked like a meteorite or a shooting star heading straight toward the house.

The sound intensified, outrumbling the thunder. Arf ran to the corner of the porch and barked like crazy.

Then he saw it. An airplane screaming down, blocking out the sky. It hit the ground at a shallow angle, cut across the fields like a plowshare, rending a deep gash in the earth. It skidded toward the house and, as if meant to dock there, slid to a stop, no more than an arm's length from the second-floor bedroom window.

The air stank of jet fuel and the hot skin of the plane sizzled as it cooled in the rainfall. He worried if anyone was alive inside the huge aircraft when the emergency door popped open and an inflatable orange chute unfurled. Two men in jumpsuits scooted down the slide, their movements herky-jerky in the jagged light of the storm.

One of the men introduced himself as the captain and asked to use the phone. The second man, the copilot, drank some water, petted Arf, and said, "Oh man, oh man" a few dozen times. The storm was the worst he'd ever seen. He couldn't believe he was alive.

An hour later the thunderhead was just damp air and water dripping off the eaves. The two men said their good-byes and walked down the dirt drive out to the road. It was as if they'd just dropped in to say hi and now the visit was over.

"Hey," Wally called out. "I think you left something."

"It's all yours," the captain said. "Just a pile of junk. We were flying it to the scrapyard in Arizona. Maybe you can get something for it."

How many mornings had he awoken in his bedroom staring out at a cockpit where the sun once came up? How many days had he spent tracing the plane's great hump. How had this incredible object come to dominate his thoughts? How had he let so many acres of hay go without cutting?

He didn't know. But was absolutely certain that the lightning storm had been heaven-sent, that the 747 was a gift, a windfall, and that he had to use it in a way that would lift up his life.

When he decided to eat the plane to prove his love for Willa, he thought it would be his own private business. He never told her what he was doing—he just hoped that sooner or later she would come to know. Now hundreds of people were watching and waiting with cameras that would tell the whole wide world how he felt about Willa.

He was ready. He hauled a chunk of honeycomb sheeting over to the chute, dropped it in, and pushed the red button. The grinding noise carried across the field, and instead of turning away and ignoring the sound, as people always did, the crowd cheered.

He climbed down from the rafters and walked proudly to the front of his contraption. The great grinding sound was heard all around Nuckolls County, broadcast live to the whole country, in bedrooms and boardrooms, and beamed via satellite to every corner of the world.

Wally reached into the machine and pulled out a bucket of metal grit. He walked over to the little place that had been cleared for him in front of the press.

"Mr. Chubb, Mr. Chubb," a reporter called out to him. "Is this the first glass and metal you've ever eaten?

"Nope," he said. "When I was a boy, my ma once put a thermometer in my mouth. I swallowed it by accident, and it didn't hurt me at all." He chuckled a bit.

"Mr. Chubb," said a reporter in a fancy blue suit. Wally thought he had seen him on TV. "How long have you been eating the 747?"

"About as long as it's been in my backyard," he said.

He picked up the bucket, brandished it like a trophy, smiled for the cameras, then poured some grit into an electric blender that had been set up on a card table nearby. He added a few scoops of vanilla ice cream and some milk, pressed "blend," and made himself a thick shake.

He poured a big glass of gray sludge and raised it high into the air. He had thought long and hard about what he would say to the world, but as he gazed at Willa, the words just vanished. He let out a giant smile. This was the beginning of great things.

"Question, Wally. Over here. Why are you doing this? Why are you eating the airplane?"

Wally didn't answer. Willa was right there in the front row.

He grinned at her, then cast his eyes over this world of newfound friends. He took a gulp, burped.

"What's it taste like?" someone shouted.

"Not bad," he said. "A bit metallic. Reminds me of diet soda. Like Tab."

Then he drained the glass with a few more glugs, finishing off the 46-blade fan assembly of the 747.

CHAPTER 8

In her whole life, Rose had never seen so many flowers.

Even at the hospital maternity ward, there were never so many bouquets. These weren't the familiar carnations and pom-poms from Superior Floral. These were showy, expensive arrangements of strange, exotic blossoms, flown in from big cities, then driven all the way from Lincoln or Omaha.

She primped the flower stems and pushed her nose into the roses. They smelled fancy even in Wally's grubby living room. She poked her finger down into the stems to test the water level.

Rose had stopped by to check up on him, as she often did on her way to the hospital. She had brought along one of her prized angel food cakes, top blue winner at the State Fair in Lincoln in 1986. Wally was in the kitchen fixing lunch. Arf snoozed at his feet.

"You hear about Shrimp?" she asked.

"What?" Wally said.

"Got blown off the road again. State Patrol says it's going to yank his badge unless he puts on some weight real fast."

"Well, I saw him eat three Herfburgers at the inn yesterday," Wally said.

"Jeez. Is he trying to gain weight or kill himself?"

They both laughed. Rose opened the card on the newest bouquet. It came from a TV anchorwoman in New York. It said she admired Wally, thought he was cute, wanted to know his innermost thoughts, asked if he'd to fly to New York City, all expenses paid, for an exclusive interview.

The phone rang.

"Please hold for—" a peppy person said, too fast for Rose to understand. Then she heard an instantly recognizable voice.

"Hi there," a sultry woman said. "Who's this?"

"Rose Lofgreen," she said.

"I'm calling from New York and just wanted to make sure Mr. Chubb got our basket of fruit."

"Yup. We've got it right here."

"Well, I hope it mixes well with the airplane." She laughed. "So tell me, Rose, how can I convince him to go on my show?"

Rose looked toward the kitchen. Wally was biting into a peanut butter and wing torsion box sandwich.

"I don't think he really wants to talk to anyone right now," she said. "He's happy just the way things are."

"Are you his girlfriend? You're a very lucky lady—"

"No, I'm not," Rose said. "He doesn't have a girlfriend."

And that was the shame of it. Wally needed a woman in his life. Needed *her*. She hadn't always felt this way about him. Like everyone else, she once thought he was a great big goofball. Then she sat next to him in church one day and heard him sing "Amazing Grace." He was too loud and way off-key, but the hymn rumbled out of him from some deep place. It touched her. He got to her again at the 4-H potluck picnic when he ate nearly a whole tub of her potato salad. Later, when her marriage to Bad Bob unraveled, Wally was the one who sat her down at Jughead's and told her she'd be better off happy and alone than miserable with a bully.

Rose's divorce taught her a lot; mostly that love could start with a spark, a twirl on the dance floor, but could grow only with understanding and acceptance of the other. That true love meant knowing someone the way they know themselves. And that was why she could watch over Wally, love Wally, even as he pined for Willa. It wasn't easy. Especially now with an acre of flowers in his living room, each petal, every single bloom, encouraging him to keep going down exactly the wrong road.

"But I thought—" the TV woman's voice broke into her thoughts.

"I'll add your name to the list." Rose said made a note

in the composition book that was filling up with messages. She printed the woman's name next to Ted Koppel and Geraldo Rivera.

"Who's called already?"

"The phone hasn't stopped ringing."

"Should I fly out to meet him in person? A quiet dinner, maybe?" Her voice was soft and flirty.

"Not really," Rose said. "He's not that kind of guy, and you probably won't like the food."

"Well, please tell him I'd do anything to have him on the show."

"Okay, will do."

And she hung up.

"Who was that?" Wally asked, entering the living room.

"Just another reporter."

"Has Willa called?"

"No," Rose said. "She hasn't called."

"Did you see her?"

"No." She knew her tone was snippy; there was no hiding it.

"Hey? What's wrong?"

"I've been here all day, getting the door every ten minutes for another box of chocolates from some celebrity. I've answered phone calls from Brazil, Japan, and Germany. I'm tired, and I've got to go to work now. My shift is about to start."

"Thanks for helping," Wally said. He put his thick hand on her shoulder. "You want to take some of the flowers?"

"No," she said. "I don't want your flowers."

Rose stuck her arms through the sleeves of her white nurse's coat, buttoned it across her chest. No matter what she did—no matter how much she cared—no matter how many cakes she baked—he didn't notice her at all. She was invisible. There was no use.

"I better get to work." She lifted herself on her tiptoes and kissed him on the cheek. His beard was prickly and he smelled like damp earth.

She might as well have kissed Arf.

Willa rolled down her window and drove slowly along East Third. A crowd had gathered in front of *The Express*. The guys who usually hung out at the Gas 'N Shop or the B.S. Café at the grain elevator in Webber had converged on the curb to watch all the TV reporters. The townfolk were reveling in all the attention, beaming innocence to anyone with a mind to exploit them.

Normally she was proud to be a journalist, but today her fellow reporters looked like predators, hunting for delicious bits of flesh and blood, alert for the next story even as they picked this one clean. They didn't give a hoot about the town and its people. This was about survival, their survival. She would have no part helping any of them.

She took a right at the end of the block, parked, and walked up the narrow alley where she could watch the circus, unnoticed. She listened to a blonde with a bad dye job overemoting into the camera.

"We're here where the mystery woman works," she was saying. "All we know about Willa Wyatt is that she's the editor of this little paper. She was born in this town, educated at the University of Nebraska."

The reporter stopped midsentence.

"This wind is killing my hair," she said. "Let's do it again. Take two."

The mystery woman. Yes, indeed, she definitely needed to remember to be mysterious. The thought of it made her laugh out loud and cringe at the same time. Reporters always chased the juiciest angle. Willa slipped down the alley and entered the Superior Publishing Company building through the loading dock door.

"Where've you been?" Iola said, looking up from her desk. "You've gotten 35 telephone calls. *The New York Times* wants to talk with you."

"How's tomorrow's paper?" Willa asked, walking to the paste-up room. The pages were there, arranged neatly on the layout tables, awaiting her approval. There was the huge 60-point headline, SUPERIOR MAN EATS 747 FOR WORLD RECORD. She had to put the story on the front page, damn it. There was no choice. What else could she do?

"*The New York Times*, Willa! They want to talk with you."

"Tell Bud to hold page two for an hour. And the *Times* can read what I have to say in my editorial."

Willa closed her office door. When she needed to write fast on deadline, she usually worked with the old computer on her desk, but when the words came from the heart, she went straight to her father's Underwood No. 5. It made comforting sounds, well-worn keys striking the platen, a little bell when the carriage returned. Sure it was harder pushing those old key tops, but the effort connected her to the thoughts flowing from her mind and hands.

She rolled a clean sheet of paper into the old typewriter. For a long while, she stared at the photograph on the wall—a streak of lightning in a black sky—then she began to type.

First, a simple headline in 36 point: WELCOME TO SUPERIOR.

Then the text.

> What makes Superior great? It's not a giant ear of corn, a beer drinking goat, or a man eating a 747. For more than 100 years, in good times and bad, we've worked the land, kept faith with God, and helped our neighbors. That's what's superior about Superior.

She hit return on the carriage and the bell rang.

> Let's make sure that when the circus leaves town—as it inevitably will—we've kept hold of what's really important. You all know that *The Express* has never written about Wally Chubb and the 747 before. His decision to eat the plane and his reason for doing so always seemed private to us. They still do.
>
> But now that the story is out, and the world has rushed here to witness the event, we can't very well look the other way. So, we'll cover the story—the runs, hits, and errors, if you will. But we'll leave it at that. No psychoanalysis. No up-close and personal features. Just the facts.

Almost done. One last line, then the presses could roll.

> So welcome to Superior, everyone. We have one simple request: that you get to know us for who we really are, not for what one man wants to eat.

A greasy, untidy fellow rushed through the front door of the bowling alley. His stringy black hair was pasted over from one side of his head, sprayed to his skull. He wore a rumpled brown corduroy suit and a red tie. His nervous eyes scanned the room. He twitched with the crash of balls striking pins.

It was league night. Farmers and wives filled the long and narrow hall. Echoes bounced from the four walls— shouts, laughter, the boom of balls skidding down maple and pine. Then the stranger saw Wally in lane six, the graveyard of Superior Bowl, with a lone fluorescent tube sputtering overhead. For the first time ever, the manager had urged Wally to take a better lane, but after spending his whole life on the margins, he wasn't about to go moving up now. While the Superior Motor Parts team whooped it up under the lights in lane five, Wally lofted his ball alone in semigloom.

The stranger scampered over outstretched legs and bowling bags and charged toward Wally with business card in hand.

"Mr. Chubb?"

"Name's Wally," he said. He lowered his Brunswick Zone Pro with extra-wide holes, custom-drilled in Grand Island to accommodate his fingers. He took the card.

"Orson Swindell," the man said. "I'm with Procter & Gamble. We make Pepto-Bismol."

The salesman smelled of hard liquor and Aqua Velva.

"It's an honor to meet you, Wally." He drew a long

breath. "I won't take up your time. Remember the McCaughey septuplets in Iowa? Pampers and Gerber's owned them lock, stock and diapers. You're going to be bigger. Much bigger!"

He wheezed.

"I'm here to offer you $100,000, cash up-front, in exchange for exclusive sponsorship of your, uh, your plane-eating activities."

Swindell drew an imaginary banner in the air. "'Pepto-Bismol!" he said. "If you go to far with your 747, the one that coats is the one that soothes." He snorted at his own inventiveness.

"Just curious," Wally said. "What makes Pepto-Bismol pink?"

"Good question." As Swindell launched into a discourse on red dyes No. 22 and 28, Wally began to do the arithmetic. One hundred thousand dollars up-front. One hundred grand for what he had been doing for free. He wouldn't make that much in 10 years even if corn prices went up. Heck, it was more money than he could make plowing the entire state of Nebraska. One-quarter would pay off the second mortgage on the farm. Another quarter would buy a decent combine and planter. The remainder would make a fine nest egg for his old age—his and Willa's.

"I personally think Pepto should be turquoise," Swindell was saying. "It's more soothing."

Wally turned to a small wrinkled man sitting under the light at the scoring table. He was swathed in a blue haze of smoke. "Otto, what do you think of Mr. Swindell's offer?"

Otto Hornbussel was 96. A retired Carson & Barnes circus clown with bright green eyes, pink cheeks, and wisps of white hair standing on end, he looked every bit an elf. He took a long quaff of red beer, belched delicately, and patted his lips with a blue bandana.

"Par for the course," Otto said. He puffed on an un-filtered Camel and squinted at a separate score sheet on his table, a careful tally of all the sponsorship offers from day one.

"Folks at Tums offered 75 grand," he said. "Maalox offered 150, but only if you get the record. Gas-X hasn't come back with its final proposal yet." He ran his finger down the growing list of bidders in the upset stomach and heartburn category: Rolaids, Mylanta, Ex-Lax, Gaviscon, Pepcid AC, Tagamet B, Zantac.

He turned the page to all the other bids. "Course Black and Decker offered 200, and they guarantee TV appearances in their commercials." He coughed. "Cuisinart is talking about 250, but you'd have to go to France too."

Wally went back to the foul line, like a giant playing Skeeball. The 16-pound ball seemed miniature in his powerful hand. He lifted it up and let loose with a sweeping, graceful motion. He turned his back, listening to the smack of the pins.

Strike.

"Strike it rich!" Orson Swindell shouted. "We'll double the offer. $200,000. Strike it rich."

Wally grinned. In his mind, he had planted a whole section of his land, sprinkling the cash and sponsorships like corn seed over every bump in his fields. Then in the end, he decided it would only dirty what was pure and simple, his true north. He waved good-bye to the two hundred grand.

"Thanks for your offer," he said, "but I don't want your money and I don't need your Pepto-Bismol. Love's good enough for me."

Otto crumpled up his list of corporate sponsors and tossed it in the trash.

"That's my Wally," Otto said, penciling a fat black X in the tenth and final frame. "You're the champ."

In comforting darkness, Willa worked, relishing the smell of sodium thiosulfate in the fixer bath, the steady drip of the sump pump in the corner of the damp photo lab. Making pictures for *The Express* had always been her favorite job, and this basement had been her hideaway, a cool retreat on summer days, a good place to go when life got crazy.

No phones. No farm bulletins. No hassles. There, in the belly of the building, she could focus, make pictures, and think. No fancy meditation. Just a way to find clarity . . .

So after dinner and dishes at her best friend Rose's, and a good drubbing on *Jeopardy*, she hopped in the old Ford and rushed back to work.

She had shot a whole roll of film that day at Wally's kick-off, developed the negatives that afternoon, and now 36 exposures awaited her on the drying line, shiny strips of truth. All night, she had wanted to get back to the darkroom, to run the enlarger, to look, to know.

She flipped on the safelight and a soft orange glow spread over the room. She slipped the last smooth sheet of developing paper into stop bath, then fixer.

The stairs creaked. Footsteps. Who could it be at this hour?

"Barney?" she called out to her pressman. "That you?"

No reply. More footsteps, then five knocks on the dark-room door. Five beats in distinctive rhythm. For 25 years, their secret code to the clubhouse.

"Dad!" she said. "You scared me."

"Coast clear?"

"Come on in."

"Evening," Early Wyatt said, slipping through the door. "Knew I'd find you—"

"What's up?" she said. No doubt, he was already in bed when Mae roused him to go look for her. His black hair was a bit askew, his sharp eyes sleepy. His pajama top was well hidden beneath his Royals windbreaker. Only the slippers gave him away.

"Your mother's trying to find you," he said.

He looked past her, toward the enlarger and the photographs in the developing trays. "Everything okay? What's so important at this hour?"

"Just wanted to get a head start on the paper tomorrow—"

"Let's see what you've got—"

"No, Dad," Willa said, stepping between her father and the developing trays. Before she had a chance to stop him, he was already pushing the tongs into the chemicals, pulling out the wet pictures.

He shook them out, then attached them with pins to

the drying line. More than a dozen black-and-white photographs. Then he stood back and looked. So many images of the man from *The Book of Records*. Different angles of J.J. Smith. Close up. Far away. Smiling. Serious. An arm around Wally. A hand on the lapel of his blue blazer.

"He's got a good face," Early said. "Friendly eyes. And my gosh, what a straight nose."

"Think I'll use this one for page one," she said in a voice that wasn't nearly as professional as she intended. "Three columns, above the fold. What do you think?"

Early was quiet for a long time, and she knew he was looking straight through her.

"Used to come down here with rolls of film when I was courting your mother," he said finally. "Made pictures of her all night long. Then you showed up, and I spent even more time here, looking at the two of you. My girls."

"It's nothing like that," she said, flipping on the lights. "It's for page one."

"Sure," he said.

"I'm raising the press run and adding to the stuffing crew. Going for another 2,000 papers. Can't keep up with demand."

"That's good. Don't print too many. You know what I always say. They just end up—"

"End up on the bottom of someone's bird cage," she said.

They both laughed.

"It's bedtime," he said. "Night, child."

He kissed her on the cheek, hugged her as hard as he could, then whispered, "You don't have to hide behind your press pass with me."

CHAPTER 9

The tour buses from Dallas and Chicago
dumped the city folk right at the corner
of Fourth and Central. Cameras slung
around necks, Nebraska maps in hand,
they were greeted by peddlers hawking
747 T-shirts. One design featured Wally's
giant face, mouth wide open, biting two
buns with lettuce, tomato, and an airplane in between.

In front of the Ideal Market, Mrs.
Hilda Crispin, who had toiled for years
in the bakery, was now making serious
dough with her very own *Jumbo Jet
Cookbook* featuring local recipes. Across
the street, Superior Floral was raking it
in with boutonnieres and hand-painted
ribbons that said: Go Wally!

And in the empty lot around the corner, Ace Klinker was chopping up his beloved single-engine crop duster into tiny pieces. He had wrecked the sprayer on his last drunken flight when he tried to land and smashed into a stop sign on the edge of town. To anyone with the stomach, Ace was now offering a bite of a real airplane.

Willa thought she could hear the cash registers waking up the town. She put the green Ford into reverse and checked the rearview mirror when someone rapped on the window.

J.J. Smith. The guy who started it all. Damn, that blue buttondown was made for those eyes.

"Hey there," he said, leaning on the hood. "How you doing?"

"Pretty good," she said. "I'm on the delivery run. Dropping off papers."

"Mind if I tag along?"

"It's not very interesting. I've got to shoot down to Mankato. Takes a good hour or so round trip."

"I'd enjoy that," he said.

She hesitated for an instant, but he seemed so eager. She nodded toward the passenger seat. "Okay, toss that bundle in the back."

J.J. threw the newspapers into the flatbed, then climbed in beside her. He looked happy. That little smile at the corners of his mouth made him seem almost—well, cute. Then she remembered: don't think that way. Blue eyes be damned. This man could be the enemy.

"This old Ford doesn't ride as smooth as you're used to," she said, pulling out onto Central. "My dad bought it new in '67 and it's been hauling papers ever since. Can't bear getting a new one. Just turns money into rust. though I could use new shocks."

In silence, they drove south of town, across the Republican River and over the state line into Kansas. Willa mulled over topics of conversation, rejected each one as too combative or inane. She turned on the radio and shut it off again when the reception turned to static. J.J. seemed content to stare out at land, so she named the crops, the owners of the farmhouses, and pointed out the soaring red-tailed hawks in the sky.

At the crest of a long, gentle incline, Willa pulled over to the side of the road.

"I love this spot," she said. "Take a look back. You can see all of Superior."

The two got out and stood at the edge of a gentle slope. The sky was a clear cornflower blue and the air smelled of new hay. Down below in the valley, they could see the little town decked out in its newfound colors. Balloons floated from lampposts. Banners dangled over the streets. Two propeller planes circled above.

Willa pointed to the east. "See over there? That's where I grew up. The white Victorian on the edge of town. The one with the windmill."

"It's beautiful," J.J. said.

"When I was a kid, my dad used to stop here on the paper run," Willa continued. "We used to drink a Coke and take a long look at the valley. You can tell who's farming well. Who's adding on to his home. You can know so much about this place from up here. I loved running papers with my dad and learning about this valley."

She was talking an awful lot, enjoying playing tour

guide. She knew what she wanted—to make this man understand this place.

"I used to drive with my dad too," J.J. said. "He marked roads for the Ohio Department of Transportation. He used to let me mix and heat the paint, even spray it on asphalt. At the end of a good stretch, we'd stop and look back at what we'd done. 'Those lines put order in people's lives,' he used to say. Then he'd slap me on the head. 'No stopping now, kid, there's always more road ahead.'"

Willa imagined J.J. as a boy, helping his dad paint stripes on those endless roads. She felt a wee bit of jealousy, that he had gotten himself out of the Midwest, broken free of his roots and seen the world. And yet she felt a kindred connection—they both came from nowhere, grew up in the back of trucks with their fathers, and learned what really mattered in life.

"This your favorite spot?" J.J. was asking.

"It's pretty special," she said, "but the best is right over there." She pointed to a bend in the river. "See those cottonwood trees. I've spent whole summer days down there by the water. Safest place in the world to escape."

"So how does the town look now?"

She shook her head. "Different."

"Different bad? Or different good?"

"Too soon to tell," she said.

J.J. smiled. "It'll only get better."

She ran her hand over her neck and felt the moisture. Then she pulled her hair up over her head to cool off. It wasn't just the heat of late afternoon. It was the feeling, surprising and inescapable, that she liked him. Simple as that. She turned to face him. "I guess you've seen this happen before."

J.J. shrugged. "More than once. On more than one continent."

"You like to travel?" she asked.

"Sure, but I get bored pretty fast if I stay too long. How about you?"

"Been to Lincoln," she said. "More than once."

They both laughed. She wondered how fast he would get bored with Superior. How soon would he move on? Would he even wait for Wally to finish off the plane?

"I can imagine you in other places," he said.

She gave him a sneak of a smile. "Like where?"

"Like a little café in Santa Margherita Ligure."

"Where's that?" she said.

"Italy. A village on the water. I can see you drinking Asti and all the waiters fighting over you."

"Asti Spumante?"

"Sort of," he said. "Asti de Miranda. World's best fizz. That's not an official record, but it's my favorite. Smells like apricots, figs, even a bit of sage. Tastes creamy, like heaven."

Willa dipped her eyes. All this talk about Italy and bubbles. Was he trying to impress her? Or was he coming on to her? She tucked a strand of hair behind her ear. Wished she had on better jeans, not the ones frayed across the knees.

"I've always wanted to see Italy," she said.

"You ever think about leaving Nebraska?" he asked.

"Not really." Her thoughts were coming quickly now. It

was a familiar fantasy spun out in her daydreaming since childhood. A worldly man—like J.J. Smith—would sweep her off her feet and take her away from Superior. Where they ran—their destination—never really mattered.

"Going away to college was a good thing," she said, "but my roots are here. I belong here." She dropped her hair from above her head and it tumbled down over her shoulders. "God, that sounds boring."

"Not boring. But I never understood people afraid to leave home."

"I'm not afraid."

"Okay. But don't you want to see the ocean? Stand on top of a skyscraper? Drink sparkling wine in an outdoor café?"

What could she say that wouldn't make her seem like a hayseed? Was he getting personal because he was interested? Or was he just messing with her head?

"Shucks, mister. How far can you go on a tractor?"

"You'd be surprised," he said. "World record is 14,500 miles. England to Zimbabwe."

"Very funny," she said. "Time to go." She opened the truck door, climbed up, and started the engine as J.J. got back in. They drove a few miles, then Willa broke the silence.

"Don't you ever get homesick?"

"Nope," he said. "I don't have a home the way you mean it."

"What about New York?"

"That's more like home base. I get mail there and keep a change of clothes."

"Where's your family?" she asked.

"My folks are gone," he said. "Happened a long time ago—"

"I'm sorry—"

"It's fair to say my whole life is The Book. The record holders are my family."

She looked over at him, noticed his frayed collar. No one in the world to take care of him. She wanted to see into his eyes, to know him better, but he squirmed in his seat and stared out the window, away from her.

"Have you ever tried to set a record?" she asked, hoping to bring him back.

"Nah," he said. "No point."

"Why not?"

"I just verify them. I don't break them."

"Ah. And why is that?"

He put his hand out the window and spread his fingers to the wind. "I stay in my own lane and measure greatness in other people."

"But don't you want to make your own mark?"

The truck rattled toward Mankato. He was quiet for so long Willa wondered if she'd been rude.

"J.J.?"

"I don't have it in me," he said finally. "I'm not that kind of guy."

Willa pondered his words for a few moments. Then, she said softly, "Come on, what're you afraid of?"

The egg wobbled through the air, end over end, catching the sun for an instant, glowing translucent gold. J.J.

reached out and felt the shell shatter in his fingers. Cool, slimy goo dripped down his arm.

In all his years with The Book, he had never once tried to break a record. Sure, there were plenty of opportunities. Wing walking was definitely the easiest: 3 hours and 23 minutes. Roy Castle set the mark by strapping himself to the wing of a plane and flying from England to France. With enough rope, resolve, and tranquilizers, anyone could topple that record. It would take only 3 hours and 24 minutes.

Now, because of an irrepressible woman, J.J. stood in a cornfield with three cartons of fresh eggs. Far and away, his favorite category in The Book had always been "Projectile Throwing." Specifically, the egg toss. Long dominated by the Finns, the record was now held by Americans, 323 feet 2½ inches without breaking the egg. Johnny Dell Foley threw a fresh hen's egg to Keith Thomas in Jewett, Texas. J.J. had been there.

After dropping off the last newspapers, he and Willa had spent a good half hour at Kier's Thriftway in Mankato debating the aeronautical merits of the different sizes. As a nod to scientific inquiry, they settled on three—medium, large, and jumbo. They also bought a roll of paper towels and a bottle of cheap white wine.

The sun was setting and a gorgeous warm light blessed the fields. J.J. had marched 109 generous paces, well beyond the record, just to show Willa how far 323 feet really was.

"Hellooooooo," he called from the far side of the field.

She waved to him. He could see her smile a full football field away. She was barefoot in a yellow sundress, and she stretched in the wind.

"You sure you want to do this?" he called out.

"Yeah," she said. "Quit stalling!"

"Fine." He jogged back to her. "Let's take this in degrees. Say we try 15 feet for starters."

"You're on," she said.

As she counted off 15 steps, she laughed like a young girl. She turned toward him, her dress flitting in the wind. He liked her face when she wasn't accusing him of ruining Superior. He took off his shirt and threw it in the fork of an elm tree. He saw her watching and he sucked in his belly. He wished he did more sit-ups and push-ups.

"Shake 'em up good," he said. "Break up the yolk and they fly better."

"Here comes a jumbo," she said, throwing it underhand.

The first few were easy and their confidence grew. Back and forth they threw gently, catching, missing, laughing. Impatiently they increased the distance, first 40, then 60 feet. Eggs cracked in their palms, goo flew everywhere.

"This isn't fair," Willa said. "How come I'm getting yuckier than you?"

"I'm plenty messy," he said.

They looped eggs high in the air. Pop, one on Willa's head.

"Ow," she yelled. "The mediums hurt. They're like golf balls."

Splat, another against J.J.'s chest. Egg splooge dribbled down his stomach.

"Willa," he called, flicking shells from his skin. "You throw like a girl. Bigger the arc, easier to catch."

She zinged one straight at him, whizzing by his head.

"Whoa! No fair!"

"Yes, fair," she said. "Shortstop. Nuckolls County All Stars. Four years in a row."

She threw another egg, overhand, muscles flexing in her arm. She was holding back all along. He should have known better. He tossed the egg back to her, a wild throw, and she lunged for it, legs tensing, dress lifting a few precious inches. He was certainly no match for her, and he could barely concentrate. The sight of her, pirouetting in the field, was dazzling. He felt drunk with whimsy, and afraid the buzz would wear off.

"Trust me," she said. "If you let your hand swing with the egg when you catch it, it cushions the impact."

"You do it your way. I'll do it mine," he said. "Here we go. 100 feet."

His hand was slippery and he raised his arm to throw. He felt the yolk move as he let it go. A high throw.

She leaped up in a swirl of yellow and gold, caught the egg in her fingertips, and landed. She raised a fist triumphantly.

"Yessss!"

They tossed eggs until the last one had flown and crashed, and they both dripped with goop. The ground was speckled with 36 yellow splotches ringed with white shards.

"So?" she said. "How'd we do?"

"Sorry," J.J. said, his sticky face all somber. "No record."

They cleaned up with the paper towels and a bottle of water. They stood inches apart, wiping goo off each other. She smelled salty and sweet. He found specks of shell in her cascading curls and gently mopped yolk from her back. He felt her warmth, her muscles, and then the faint shudder of her whole body when he brushed egg bits from the silky hairs on her neck.

Then they flopped down in the field to watch the sun go down, throwing great and glorious splashes of plum across the clouds. Willa's skin was luminous, her eyes gleaming. Even the toenails on her dusty bare feet seemed to twinkle, each one painted pink.

She opened the bottle of wine with the corkscrew on her pocket knife. They had forgotten glasses so they passed the bottle back and forth and took great swigs.

J.J. knew the giddy feeling inside him. During his extensive interviews with scientists about the nature of love, he had nailed the formula: Attraction was a chemical reaction, nothing more. His midbrain was pumping dopamine, norepinephrine, and phenylethylamine. His pheromones, invisible airborne molecules of scent, were flying. And her brain was firing, too. The signs were there. Her skin was covered with a light mist of sweat, her eyes dilated, her face was flushed.

He felt confused. Science had always made him feel safe, impervious, but what had happened? Just days ago he had left Paris grousing about love. Now, despite his ratios and equations, more than anything in the world, he wanted this woman, wanted to know her, wanted to bury himself in her. But then, like a beaker breaking in the lab, he remembered. This was business . . .

When he spoke, he was surprised that his voice sounded almost normal. "So," he said, "I have to ask you. What's your relationship with Wally Chubb?"

CHAPTER 10

Shrimp eased his patrol car behind the
beat-up '68 VW van with Oregon plates.
The driver of the suspect vehicle had
long red hair and a matching Moses
beard. He had pulled into town that
morning, accompanied by two dark-eyed
women who—sources claimed—weren't
wearing brassieres. They stopped at the
grocery store, then spent the day inside
the van, curtains pulled shut. There was
nothing illegal about it, but everyone
was keeping a close eye on them.

On this fine Sunday evening, as the
good folks of Superior sat down for supper, the long-haired man was driving
through town in his van with a loud-

speaker, shouting something about the Messiah, the 747, and technology.

This hippie was disturbing the peace, and Shrimp definitely had to do something about it.

The man pulled over to the side of the road. Shrimp got out of the squad car, inflated his chest as best he could, and strutted toward the VW.

"License, please," Shrimp said.

The man with the long hair smelled terrible. The women in the backseat were barely dressed.

"What's the problem, man?" the hippie asked.

"Disturbing the peace," Shrimp said. "That's the problem."

"I've got a right to free speech."

"You sure do, son. But in Superior, you can't go around blasting your loudspeaker like that. It's against the law."

"What law?"

"I am the law, son. Get out of the vehicle."

A small crowd had gathered to watch. The hippie climbed out of the van. There were gasps as everyone realized the man was wearing no pants, no shorts, only a tie-dyed shirt and hiking boots. The women followed him, fully clothed, so to speak.

"Wake up, people, before it's too late!" the man shouted. "Technology is destroying society!"

Shrimp led the three hippies to the patrol car.

"Wally is our savior," the man screamed as he was shoved into the back seat. "Eat the Plane! Eat technology. Eat evil."

•　　•　　•

The streetlights threw circles on the pavement. Willa stopped the truck to drop J.J. off. She had barely pulled away when reporters surrounded him. Then he was swept away with the crowd.

She drove down East Third, turned right on Central, then cruised to the front of the Lady Vestey Center. The whole time, she picked apart her answer to J.J.'s question:

What's your relationship with Wally?

"I've known him all my life," she had said. "He's not normal and easy to figure out. Even when he was young, he was this huge, uncomfortable guy. He didn't have friends. I liked him, though. He has a good heart.

"I think he got this crush when I went to his tenth birthday party. I thought it would go away, but it didn't," she said. "He's always had a shine for me. I see him once in a while in town. But now he's really blown this way out of proportion. Well, that's my opinion."

"I think I understand," J.J. said.

She hoped he really did understand. She liked Wally, but she never imagined ending up with him. And right now she wanted to clink glasses of Asti de Whatever with this man who knew the world.

The Lady Vestey Center was as grand as government funding could make it. Once an old hotel, it was now a nursing home for the elderly, named for its benefactress, Evelyn Brodstone, a native daughter who left Superior and married British nobility.

Willa walked through the large hall, her sandals clacking on the terrazzo floor, past the darkened lounge and deserted coffee corner. At last, she found Rose washing up in the ladies' room. She was just finishing up her part-time job caring for residents of the center.

"What happened to you?" Rose asked. "What's that in your hair?"

"You won't believe it," Willa said. "You won't believe what I just did."

"Try me." Rose handed her friend a towel. Willa scrubbed her face and rinsed her hair in the sink.

They walked back to the lounge, a room with a dozen chairs. A large TV played in the corner, running the local news. Willa and Rose took two Barcaloungers.

"I spent the afternoon with the guy from *The Book of Records*," Willa said. "We went out to Righty's field and tried to break the record for tossing eggs. It was a riot. We laughed our asses off."

"You tried what?"

"Projectile throwing. You know, the egg toss. We didn't come close to the record." Willa could hear herself—her voice all dizzy.

"You're putting me on," Rose said.

"Honest," she said.

"What's going on?"

"Nothing. Nothing! Why are you looking at me like that?"

"You should see yourself, Willa. You're goo-goo-eyed."

"That's crazy! I just had a great day. Played all afternoon. Haven't done that in ages. Nothing to worry about."

"You're going to do it all over again, aren't you? The last time you got carried away, it took two years to get back to normal."

"We were only playing. That's all, I swear."

Rose shook her head.

"It's been so long since I had any fun," Willa said softly. "And it's been even longer since I felt anything."

"You know nothing about him."

Willa showed her open palms. Nothing to add. She stared at her friend.

"Nuts," Rose said quietly. "Honestly, Willa."

A tiny old man in a blue pajamas, white hair sticking up on his head, got up from a La-Z-Boy and shuffled over to the television. He took a cigarette out of his mouth. "You ladies mind?" he asked.

"No, go ahead," said Rose. "We're not watching."

Otto Hornbussel changed the television station to CNN.

"Look," said Rose.

An anchorman with shellacked gray hair was saying: "Joining us live tonight, J.J. Smith of *The Book of Records*. Tell us, what's really going on out there in Nebraska?"

"Evening," J.J. began. "This one's a real doozie . . ."

Behind him, a bunch of teenagers made rabbit ears for the camera and waved their Budweiser cans. A few banners touting Weight Watchers and Alka-Seltzer flapped in the background. Superior was turning into a freak show.

Willa remembered what J.J. had said to her just hours ago: "My whole life is The Book." She stared at him on the screen. What a disreputable scene. Her racing heart stumbled, and slowed. He wasn't Asti de Miranda; he was Dr. Pepper. . . .

"There you go," said Rose. "Your basic, here-today,

gone-tomorrow kind of guy. I ask you: Would you buy a used car from that man?"

Willa flinched, then said, "I really hate it when you're right."

J.J. sat on a folding chair next to his friend, the famed omnivorous Frenchman Michel Lotito. With a flat nose and messy black hair, Lotito held a Gitanes cigarette in one hand and a Heineken in the other. He had been placed on a rich CNN retainer to offer expert commentary on the gastronomic challenges of eating a 747.

It was just after 9 P.M. and Wally's field was so studded with television klieg lights that it was as bright as morning. Every insect in Nuckolls County seemed to fly into the light beams. From his seat, J.J. could see all the brightly colored tents that had sprung up in the barnyard and beyond. A little one-engine crop duster flew out of the dark into the bright blaze, dragging a banner: THE GINSU: CUTS ANY METAL, EVEN A 747.

An audio technician adjusted J.J.'s ear piece.

"Hey, man," he said, "you've got something on your ear."

J.J. picked eggshell from his lobe. He felt giddy. He knew it was an electrical signal from his left prefrontal cortex. Yes, his brain was saturated with neurotransmitters. The flood of endorphins was causing strong feelings of attachment. He wanted to go back to that field with Willa, smother her with eggs, even try to set another world record, the kind that wasn't suitable for The Book.

"One minute," the audio technician whispered, "and we're on the air."

The instruction jolted him into the moment. A national television audience awaited. Time to sell. The camera's red light flashed.

"Mr. Lotito," the anchorman intoned. "A question from a caller in Raleigh. What's worse, the airplane or the airplane food?"

The Frenchman grinned. "Trust me, rubber tires taste worse than burnt lasagna. The flavor is terrible and you have to drink so much water just to get them down."

"What about metal?" the anchorman asked.

"It leaves absolutely no taste going down," Lotito said. "But later, when you burp, it's definitely metallic. As long as you pulverize the metal or sand off the sharp edges, there is no danger of lacerating your organs. You simply pass the metal without absorbing it into your system. The biggest problem is rust in your toilet."

The anchorman smothered a chuckle and tried to look unfazed. "Is it true you once ate a table setting at a restaurant in Normandy?"

"Yes, plates, glasses, forks, knives, everything."

"No problem at all?"

"The tablecloth is the worst," Lotito said. "If you don't watch out, it can clog your throat."

"Is there anything you can't eat?" the anchorman asked.

"To tell you the truth, bananas and eggs make me sick," he said.

The anchorman turned to his next guest, Dr. Hamilton Gee from the Centers for Disease Control. A bony faced man with gray filmy skin, he looked like a cadaver.

"Michel is absolutely correct," Dr. Gee said. "Metal is inert. It passes straight through the digestive tract too fast to be absorbed in the system."

"So it's perfectly safe?" the anchorman asked, incredulous.

"No, it's not safe, but it's probably less dangerous than smoking cigarettes every day or drinking in excess. Still, my bottom line: No one should eat metal without proper supervision. It could be deadly."

"It's true," Lotito said. "I hemorrhaged six pints of blood after eating a grocery cart and ten-speed bike."

"Are you afraid," the anchorman asked, "of losing your record to Wally Chubb?"

"May the best man win," said Michel. His smile was more a grimace, showing two rows of gnarled teeth, badly stained and ground down.

"We're running out of time," the anchor said. "Last question goes to J.J. Smith."

The camera panned across the bare bones of the 747, then cut back to J.J. He hoped Willa was watching the broadcast and that she would be impressed.

"Do you think Wally will be able to put away the entire jumbo jet?"

"No doubt in my mind," J.J. said. "I'll bet everything I have in the world that he'll finish this plane."

First came barking, then the beam of a flashlight on his bedroom window.

"Mr. Chubb," a man's voice called out from below. "We need to speak with you. It's urgent."

Arf growled in the shadows downstairs by the door.

In his red one-piece pajamas, Wally flipped the switch for the back porch light. He peeked through the curtains and saw a gray-suited man, square-jawed, with Ray-Ban aviator glasses and neatly combed hair. Three other grim-faced suits lurked behind him on the steps.

Sunglasses at 1 A.M. What the heck was going on? He cracked open the door.

"Mr. Chubb? Sorry about the hour." The man's voice was deep, gravelly. His Ray-Bans reflected the bare light bulb overhead. "We don't want to create a disturbance. We want to be discreet. Just need a minute of your time."

"What's the problem?"

"You sure you want to talk out here?" the man explained. "Or could we go inside?" Only a few lights were still on in Wally's field, the tents all quiet, the journalists asleep.

"What do you want?"

"We're from Boeing," the man said, "and we're here to help."

"No kidding," Wally said. "Come on in. Place is a bit messy, but make yourselves comfortable."

He put Arf into the pantry with a Milk-Bone and returned to his kitchen table. The men stood in a semi-circle. A lone black file folder lay on the counter.

"We'd like you sign this waiver," the man with the Ray-Bans said, producing a form in triplicate. "We don't put warning labels on our jets. You know, 'The surgeon general has determined that eating an airplane is hazardous to your health.' Our legal department wants you to sign this document acknowledging Boeing is not liable for any damage—

"You don't have to worry about me," Wally said. "I'm not suing anybody."

"Then you won't mind signing—"

"Sure, I'll sign it, but what do I get in return?"

"Technical assistance," the man said.

"How's that?"

The man held up a cardboard tube. "My colleagues here are 747 engineers. They designed the plane you're eating."

A roll of blueprints slid out and a schematic of the 747 unfurled onto the table.

"We're truly impressed with what you've accomplished," a Boeing engineer said, meticulously weighting down the four corners of the diagram with coffee mugs from the sink. His eyes were sincere. He was in awe of Wally.

"But you've got a big problem," the engineer said, tapping the blueprint with his forefinger. "Look here." Wally leaned closer.

It was a spot just behind the rear cabin near the tail. He hadn't eaten that far yet. But it was right around the corner.

"That's your challenge," the engineer said. Tap-tap went the finger. "It's what we call a showstopper."

A sinewy hand extended, offering a big expensive pen.

"Sign our waiver," the man with the Ray-Bans said, "and we'll help you. We know just the guy to call. Otherwise, you're on your own and you'll never finish the plane."

Why had no one thought of this before?

J.J. felt nauseated. So much work and effort would come to nothing if the problem couldn't be solved. He walked across Wally's fields, past the television booths, hot dog stands, snow cone vendors, and fortune tellers. The pasture buzzed with talk of Wally's insurmountable challenge.

He stopped briefly at the MSNBC tent where an expert from *Aviation Week & Space Technology* held a scale model of the 747 in his hands. With great consternation, he pinpointed the showstopper.

"He's conquered the avionics," the Ph.D. intoned. "He's made a run right through the undercarriage and the cargo holds. Now he faces the impossible—"

J.J. winced and moved on to the Australian Broadcasting Corporation booth where an animated discussion was under way about putting a small camera inside Wally's intestines for an in-depth exploration of his digestive tract.

He shoved his hands into his pockets and crossed over to the stark remains of the 747. He stared up at the tail section, the empennage as someone called it, waiting to be consumed. Somewhere inside that sleek aluminum skin was a showstopper, a problem with no obvious solution, an obstacle that would put an end to Wally's world record attempt . . .

The black box.

Indestructible, built to withstand 3,400 Gs or sudden impact at 400 miles per hour. How would Wally eat it if his magic machine couldn't grind it? J.J. knew this was a crisis the news media would milk for days. It would be the number-one question asked around the world.

And yet, for some mysterious reason, Wally remained confident and carefree, not worried a bit. The black box, he seemed to think, was a piece of cake.

CHAPTER 11

The Russian reeked of booze and cigarettes. His eyes were bloodshot, his
words slurred. J.J. gamely tried to answer
his unintelligible questions about the
chorny yashchik, the black box. After all,
the drunk worked for Tass, the Russian
press agency. A big new market for The
Book.

They were holed up in J.J.'s make-
shift office in the back room of the
Git-A-Bite, when suddenly the late-
afternoon wind seemed to blow open the
front door. Willa burst into the café. Her
face was flushed.

"You've got to help," she said. "Blake
is in big trouble. He says he'll only talk
to you."

J.J. grabbed his coat, followed her out onto the street and into her truck.

"He wants to set a kite-flying record," she said, tears in her eyes. "He's been building the damn thing for a year. Hasn't stopped talking about—"

"How do you know Blake?" J.J. asked.

"He's my kid brother," she said, running a stop sign.

And then it all made sense. The Guy Who Knows was Willa's little brother. Writing to The Book to help his friend Wally and his big sister. And to set a kite flying record for himself. . . .

She pulled to a hard stop.

"There!" she said, pointing across the street. J.J. looked up at the water tower, 150 feet tall, silver against the gray sky. A crowd had gathered at its base. On the metal platform at the top of the structure, Blake crouched, holding on to a big red kite with a crude body harness.

J.J. got out of the truck. Shrimp approached. His uniform was stained with sweat, his voice raspy. "Blake's a smart boy," he said. "Too smart to go jumping off the tower."

"You don't understand!" Willa said. "He thinks the wind is perfect for a flight—"

"Ain't no time for kite-flying," Shrimp said, looking east. "Storm's coming fast."

"You got a fire truck?" J.J. asked.

"No ladder that high. Need to climb up there and get him."

The chief motioned to one of his deputies. A policeman with a chest as thick as a beer keg began to climb the ladder attached to one of the massive legs of the tower.

Blake shouted from above: "Stop! Don't send anyone up here or I'll fly. I'm warning you! Don't come up." He stood up with the kite. The wind gusted. Blake struggled to put on the homemade harness attached to the kite.

"I'm going to jump," he shouted.

Shrimp called to his deputy. "Come on back, Artie. Let's wait awhile."

"No," Willa said. "Get him down."

J.J. knew there was no choice. Willa was watching. He couldn't hesitate.

"Let me give it a try," he said. He waited for the policeman to get down the ladder, and then he cupped his hands and called up.

"Blake, I'm coming up."

Without asking again, without thinking, J.J. started to climb. His arms weren't as strong as he would have liked, and the metal bars hurt his hands. With each rung, the worried whispers on the ground grew more faint. He could feel the stare of the crowd below. He couldn't let them down.

The wind whipped across his face, burning his eyes. Rung by rung, he climbed toward Blake. Twenty feet from the top, he paused to catch his breath, looked straight up, and saw the boy peering over the ledge. He knew the type—ten years old, gangly, a great gap in his front teeth, and absolutely, positively fearless.

"World record for the highest kite flight ever was 31,955 feet," J.J. shouted. "Germany, 1919." A diversionary tactic. Stall for time. "Longest recorded flight, 180 hours and 17 minutes in Long Beach, Washington."

"Cool," Blake said. "I'm gonna set a record by flying all

the way to Kansas. It's two miles. See? Jewell County is across the river down there."

J.J. looked out at the little town, grain elevator, and winding river. The boy would never make it past the railroad tracks. He started climbing again, fast.

The tower groaned in the gale, and the ladder shook. J.J.'s legs began to cramp, his hands ached. He finally pulled himself to the top and rested on the little landing at the base of the huge water tank. The rusty container was easily 20 feet tall, with great red letters painted across it: SUPERIOR WILDCATS. A rickety railing ran around the platform. Not much protection against the driving wind.

He didn't like heights. He didn't like the thunderstorm starting to sweep across the fields. And he didn't like seeing Blake—blond hair blowing wildly—struggling on the ledge with the kite.

"I know you want a record," J.J. said, moving carefully toward the boy. "But we don't recognize ones that are dangerous."

"I don't get it," Blake said, buckling the harness across his chest. "You let Wally eat a plane for my sister but you won't let me fly my kite?"

The kid had a good point. As J.J. formed a comeback, a gust of wind ripped across the tower, lifting Blake and his kite into the air, pushing them over the ledge.

J.J. lunged and grabbed Blake by the arm. The boy dangled below him, legs thrashing the air. He weighed no more than eighty pounds, but felt like eighty thousand as the wind pulled hard on the kite harnessed to his back.

"Don't drop me!" Blake screamed, his eyes huge with terror, fearlessness suddenly gone.

"Hold on!" J.J. said. His grip was giving way. Blake was slipping, gravity and the wind dragging him off. The boy's thin arm was sliding through his hand.

"I'm falling," Blake shouted. "Please—please don't let go!"

J.J. knew he could not hold back the wind. There was only one way to pull the boy to safety.

"Unhook the kite!" J.J yelled. His hand cramped from the strain. He tried to hook one leg under the railing, but the wind was dragging them both over the edge. "Now!"

Blake struggled to release the harness. "It's stuck. It won't unsnap!"

"Try again," J.J. said. "You can do it."

Blake pulled frantically on the first buckle, and finally it broke loose. Then he unfastened the second clasp and wriggled free of the shoulder straps. The kite whipped away, spiraling down. Then it caught a current and rose into the air.

"Your hands!" J.J. said. "Reach for me!"

Their fingers barely interlocking, J.J. slowly pulled the boy back up and over the ledge. They huddled up to each other, the wind pelting the platform. J.J. wrapped his arm around Blake and pulled him tight.

The two watched the kite sail higher and higher until it became just a red fleck in the silver sky. Then Blake began to cry. Voices shouted from below, muffled by the gale.

"I'm scared," he said.

"It's okay," he said. "Don't be afraid."

Blake sobbed for a long time. Then he looked up. "You ever get scared?"

A bolt of lightning flashed over the town, then came

the boom of thunder. J.J. could feel the rumbling in the air all the way to his bones. He knew each electrical charge exploded hydrogen atoms, creating a nuclear reaction with a temperature of 50,000 degrees Fahrenheit.

"Everyone's afraid of something," he said, looking at the angry sky. "Come on, we better go home."

The motel room was silent, except for the beating rain on the window. J.J. soaked in the small bathtub trying to warm up. Despite the storm, it had taken another half hour to talk Blake into going back to his sister. J.J. had made promises there would be no punishment for this escapade, assurances he would help find a safer record to set.

Back on the ground, he had caught a brief glimpse of Willa. Along with the photo she took of the rescue, she shot him a wounding look. She drove off toward *The Express* before he had a chance to talk with her. He could hear her words from Jughead's.

Don't you dare go hurting this town.

Was it his fault? Maybe she was right, after all. Maybe he wasn't the best thing to happen to Superior. Maybe Blake's adventure was just a warning sign. He had saved the boy from the tower, but he had probably lost Willa. . . .

He checked his watch. It was suppertime, but tonight there was no grinding sound from Wally's farm. No forward motion on the world record attempt. The Black Box had indeed stopped the show. All was unhappily quiet.

Then an electronic *ping* broke the silence. He got out of the bath, dripping, and found his beeper in his trousers. He recognized the dreaded phone number and made the call.

Peasley's voice was agitated, his words climbing over each other. "What's the latest?" he asked.

"Wally's machine hasn't even made a dent in the black box," J.J. said, "but he's undaunted. Claims he's got a secret plan—"

"Well, Smith, even if it doesn't work out, it may be a blessing. You see, the directors are terrified about liability. If something happens to Walter Chubb, it could wipe out The Book. You Americans are so litigious. You'll sue over anything."

"But he's fine. Nothing's going to happen to him."

"I'm in your court on this one," Peasley said. "Problem is, we've got copycats. A woman in Ghana is eating an office building. A family in Morocco is eating a bridge. A man in Malaysia is eating an ocean liner. We don't know where it will stop—"

"So what?" J.J. said. "The whole world is watching Wally. You can't cut him off now."

"Get a hold of yourself," Peasley said. "I'll talk to the directors again tomorrow. See what I can do."

"Trust me. This record will be a rare and very beautiful thing."

"Yes indeed," Peasley said. "Just keep your eye on the 747, and I'll take care of the rest."

CHAPTER 12

High above Route 14, a tight formation of news choppers followed the convoy heading north. On the ground, three patrol cars with flashing lights blazed the way for a red pickup truck. Sixty vehicles of all sizes and descriptions trailed behind, honking horns. Kids in flatbeds whooped.

Inside the red Dodge, Wally was at the wheel. His friend Nate sipped on a 7-Eleven Big Gulp.

"Pass me that, will ya?" Wally said.

Nate gave him the cup. He took a swallow and grimaced.

"This Coke tastes funny. Mind if I add some of the auxiliary power unit?"

"Be my guest," Nate said.

Wally reached under the seat and pulled out a jar filled with metal grit. He dumped some in the drink, swirled it around, and guzzled it.

"What'll you do if this doesn't work?" Nate said.

"Don't you worry. Boeing says Big Lou's the man. He'll take care of the problem. Just you wait."

Nate turned on the radio. The announcer's breathy voice filled the cab.

"If you're just tuning into KFAB, Wally Chubb's pickup is on Highway 14 just north of Clay Center. We don't know where he's going, but Nebraska and the nation wait anxiously."

Wally and Nate laughed.

The radio reporter continued: "For an eyewitness account of Wally's progress, we go live now to our Guy in the Sky, Sammy Dash in the KFAB news chopper."

Another voice cut in, this one all but overwhelmed by the racket of rotor blades and the crackle of static. "Thanks, Hank. I'm directly above the red truck right now. In the last half hour, this convoy has been gaining force. It started out as a half dozen vehicles, now it's six times that number. I can see the black box tied down in the flatbed—"

"For starters," Nate said, "the black box isn't even black. The guy must be color blind." He switched off the knob with disgust.

"I guess 'orange box' doesn't sound as good," Wally said.

"Yeah. But can't they see there are two boxes? The cockpit voice recorder and the flight data recorder?"

Wally signaled a right turn.

"What're you doing?" Nate asked.

"Gotta pee."

"On national television?"

"Guess you're right. Better not. What if Willa's watching?"

The red truck rolled along the country road. Wally loved these stretches and knew every inch and bump. Today, especially, he drank in each mile as farmers hailed him from combines and families waved from driveways.

When he reached Hastings, he began to feel a thrill himself. A glittering WELCOME WALLY! banner with red letters spanned the main entrance into town. On the steps of the old post office, the high school band boomed "When the Saints Go Marching In," and cheerleaders cartwheeled and wagged pom-poms in front of his truck.

With one meaty hand out the window, Wally flashed the victory sign at the crowds. For once in his life, he knew what it was like to quarterback the Huskers. Fans screaming your name. The biggest man in Nebraska. The most beloved.

A pimply teenage boy ran alongside the truck, then jumped on the running board.

"Hey, Wally," he said. "I ate my roller skates! Take me with you."

"Can't, son. Maybe some other time."

The boy wished him luck and hopped to the ground.

"Look at you," Nate said, "a real hero."

"If only Willa thought so," Wally said. "If only. . . ."

• • •

Luigi Cinquegrana—Big Lou—was normally the model of calm. Today he paced in small circles. Soon Wally would arrive accompanied by a small army of policemen—and Luigi did not like this intrusion. There were unanswered questions about where he got the metal he turned into scrap. Truth was that lots of times he didn't know himself. Sometimes he just handed over the shop keys to nameless clients who flew in from the East Coast. They came after hours, ran the pulverizer all night, and he never asked questions. There was always talk the next day of foul smells emanating from the scrapper, the smell of rot. There were tax problems too. But it was good money, easy money, paid in cash.

Now his worries warred with his pride in his great pulverizer. It was the best on the Great Plains. He could stick anything into that machine and it would spit out dust. And Big Lou also knew how to put on a show. When bigwigs at the Boeing factory in Wichita called around earlier in the week looking for help, Big Lou knew it meant great things for the scrapyard. So he bought his workers suits and ties, told them to get all cleaned up for the important day and to get to work on time.

The swelling sound of helicopters signaled Wally's imminent arrival. Big Lou went out to the driveway and welcomed the men in the red truck. His workers stood in a neat line behind him, their necks bursting from new collars.

"An honor to have you here," Big Lou said, as Wally got out of the truck. "We're going to make mincemeat out of the black box."

"It's orange," Wally muttered, "and there are two of them."

"Let me see the objects in question." Big Lou signaled his son, Little Lou, who ran over to the truck and released the bindings on the two boxes. They were the size of small toaster ovens, 17 pounds each. He slid them to the edge of the flatbed, lifted them up, and carried them to his father. As photographers snapped pictures, Big Lou cradled the boxes in his arms, like twin babies. Then, with Wally's approval, he jammed them into the mouth of the pulverizer.

The machine coughed, shook violently, and spewed smoke. The hydraulic parts squeezed and pushed, and the clanking sounds made people cover their ears. Audio technicians pulled off their headsets. Big Lou cranked the groaning machine to its highest gear. The orange boxes vanished.

Big Lou slapped Wally on the shoulder and marched to the other end of the pulverizer. He carried a wicker basket in one hand. He opened the little door and looked inside. Reaching in with his hand, he felt around for a moment, then stood up and looked at the row of cameras. He smiled faintly and wiped his sweaty face.

"One more minute," he said. "Just one more minute."

Then he kneeled down next to pulverizer and discreetly made the sign of the Cross. He waited for an answer from Above. And then suddenly, divinely, the machine spit out shreds of metal, curlicues of hardened-state stainless steel. They landed in the wicker basket.

Big Lou raised his eyes to the sky, then gave a signal to his team. They advanced on a great red curtain that closed off an area at the end of the yard. They yanked the veil aside. There, resplendent in shirtwaist and starched pinafore, was Mama Lou. She was surrounded by pots, pans, and huge steaming bowls of spaghetti, clams, and red sauce.

"A feast for Wally Chubb!" Mama Lou exclaimed. "*Mangia!*"

The workers carried tables and chairs into the middle of the junkyard. Reporters, cameramen, technicians threw down their gear. Even the grim men from Boeing, lurking behind great piles of scrap metal, stepped out from the shadows.

Everyone sat down as Mama Lou spooned out mountains of noodles and poured rivers of Chianti. Big Lou heaped parmesan on his pasta, while Wally sprinkled his spaghetti with fine shavings from the vanquished black box.

CHAPTER 13

A trattoria in Italy. Its name, Farfarello, in the port of Marina di Massa. Her table was covered with antipasto, smoked tuna, and swordfish. There were bowls of *vongole* salad, *tagliarini* with little shrimp, and a sprinkle of *peperoncino*. For dessert, a plate of *ciambella*. Willa had found this spot on the web. Now, with waves splashing in the harbor, she swirled Asti de Miranda in her glass. A man with soft blue eyes and a fine aquiline nose sat across from her. He leaned forward, put a hand in her hair, and pulled her toward him. . . .

She awoke with a start.

Hard fluorescent light nailed the surroundings into focus. The waiting room of Brodstone Memorial Hospital. Then the feeling of dread. . . .

Willa remembered something had gone terribly wrong in the middle of the night. Wally had collapsed in his kitchen and barely managed to dial 911. He had been rushed to the hospital in an ambulance. Rose thought it was a seizure.

Did he make it through the night? All these years, this hulking presence in town, friendly and reassuring. Always there. Always.

Why hadn't she taken him more seriously? Why hadn't she stopped him sooner? If anything happened to poor Wally, it would be her fault.

J.J. snoozed in the seat beside her. Nate stretched out on the speckled linoleum floor. Otto shambled in the hallway, trailing streams of blue smoke. Through the windows of the lobby gift shop, a purple bunny and an orange elephant stared at her. The clock on the wall said 5:55.

Out the main door, Willa could see the television trucks parked in the lot. Camera crews huddled in groups, drinking coffee, eating doughnuts. Chief Bushee stood at the front door. The vigil had gone on through the night.

There was a scuffle of footsteps coming down the hallway. Burl Grimes, funeral director and hospital board chief, walked sluggishly, shoulders stooped, expression glum, in intense conversation with a doctor.

Willa rose from her chair. Something terrible had happened. Wally was no more.

"I've got a short statement for the press," Burl said, his voice flat.

He made his way through the doors and out onto the lawn. Willa rustled J.J. and Nate. They followed outside into the bright lights where the cameras started to roll. Photographers snapped.

"Ladies and gentlemen," Burl began, "I'm here to inform you that last night—"

"Is he dead?" a reporter shouted.

"Please," he said. "I'll take questions in a minute."

He cleared his throat and began again. "Last night Wally Chubb was admitted to Brodstone Memorial after a syncopal event."

"A what?"

"A fainting episode," Burl said.

"Is it serious?"

"Doctors have completed all of their tests. On behalf of the hospital board, I can report that—"

Words beamed live around the globe. . . .

"Wally is alive and well."

A cheer erupted in the back row, then one by one, the reporters began to applaud. Willa saw Rose slip out the employee entrance of the hospital. Her braid was a mess, her eyes puffy.

"What caused the fainting?" a reporter asked.

"Dehydration and food poisoning," Grimes said. "Hard work in the fields, plus a bad clam, as best we can tell. The doctors insist this situation has nothing to do with the 747."

As Burl continued to field questions, Rose eased her way through the throng and took Willa's arm. They walked away from the crowd. Willa could feel her friend shaking.

"This was a warning," Rose said. "Wally's got to stop."

"But the doctors just said—"

"You've got to tell him to quit. You're the only one who can. He's killing himself for you."

Nate leaned back in a gray metal chair tipped against the wall of Room 239. The sunlight was bright, an old wind blew, and the rippling leaves on the big oak in the parking lot threw wavy shadows over the room. No doubt about it, Wally was fine—and that was the shame of it. Why couldn't he just stop eating the plane now, before he really got hurt?

The newspaper was lying on his blanket, the front page facing up. His smiling picture was right there and so was a story about him, written by Willa.

Wally read the headline out loud two more times: "'Superior Man Eats 747 for World Record'." Then he said, "You think she meant I'm a superior man? Or a man from Superior?"

Nate kept his silence. His best buddy was flat on his back and under the illusion—or delusion—that Willa was coming around. Truth was, the damn fool would never win Willa's heart, even if he killed himself trying.

The door opened. Doc Noojin, the town veterinarian, slipped inside. He held a finger to his lips—sssssshhhh—listened for a long moment, then went straight to Wally's bedside.

Doc was a sturdy man with a dent in his forehead from a mule kick. He had a degree in veterinary medicine from Kansas State and specialized in large animals. He was the only medical professional in the area Wally and most of the farmers trusted.

"Your color's back," Doc said. "How you feeling?"

"Never better," Wally said.

Nate leaned forward. "How'd you get in? Thought they banned you from this place."

"Rose let me in," Doc said. "Her pup Peachy is over at the clinic. She just winked and looked the other way."

He punched Wally in the arm. "In a tractor pull between you and a John Deere, I'd bet on you."

"All that hydraulic fluid better be good for something," Wally said.

"You're invincible, man. Something's protecting you, something powerful," Doc said.

Nate stood up, filled with guilt. He walked to his best friend's bedside. "I never should have helped you build the machine. Doc, you should be ashamed for encouraging him."

"Whoa," Wally said. "Slow down. This was my idea. No one else's. I'm perfectly happy—"

"Don't you see?" Nate interrupted. "This is never going to work. You'll never get what you want this way."

"What's gotten into you?" Doc said. "You need a rabies shot or something?"

"Relax," Wally said. "Everything's going according to J.J.'s plan."

"J.J.'s plan? He just wants to sell more books," Nate said. "He doesn't care about you."

"Don't worry about me," Wally said. "I know what I'm doing—"

Nate wanted to throttle his dear, deluded friend. He headed for the door; he wanted to get away before saying what would hurt, but the words spilled out.

"Face it now or face it later," he said. "You're never going to get Willa to love you."

CHAPTER 14

A little girl in pigtails and a sun bonnet rode a palomino pony down Main Street. It was a warm and bright day, perfect for the annual Memorial Day parade and Lady Vestey Festival.

J.J. was perched high in the bleachers across from Menke Drug. He watched the girl on her pony trot along the yellow line in the middle of the road. It was time her dad taught her to stay in her own lane.

Then, in his mind, he heard Peasley say, "The home office has a problem with this record." Sure, that statement had been followed by assurances that he would fight for J.J., but never had there been a bigger weasel than Peasley. J.J.

had promised the town that if Wally ate the plane, there would be a world record. And with a record, there would be a bonanza for Superior. He couldn't let them down. And he couldn't let himself down either.

"Biggest parade ever," Righty Plowden said. He was sitting beside J.J. on the metal bleachers. He wore a straw hat that looked as if a goat had feasted on a good chunk of it. "We've usually got a few flatbed trucks strung up with crepe paper ribbons, the high school band, and that's it. But today, well, this is special."

A gold '84 Cadillac convertible rolled majestically toward the intersection of Fourth and Central. Doc Noojin was at the wheel. Standing on the passenger seat, waving at the crowds, was Wally Chubb, grand marshal of the parade. Pretty young women called out "Hey, Wally," and children waved flags at the man eating the 747.

"That's one happy young fella," said Righty.

"With good reason," J.J. said.

A dozen young baton twirlers scampered down the street.

"There's my granddaughter," Righty said. "She wants to be in your book someday."

The motley high school band showed off next, followed by a sharp phalanx of WWII veterans, stepping smartly to the beat. Working his way up the sidewalk, Otto Hornbussel merrily made twisty balloon animals for the children.

Small-town America on a national holiday. The steady throb of anxiety about the world record dissipated for a moment. J.J. munched on caramel popcorn and remembered this same sunny feeling as a boy in Ohio. The parade always launched a long seamless stretch of summer. But he knew this nostalgia was just a passing whimsy. He could only take so much of a small town before he'd hunger for Manhattan, carbon monoxide, skyscrapers, and the energizing effect of 1.5 million of people living on top of each other.

"Coming to the dance?" Righty asked.

"Don't know about any dance."

"Tonight at the Elks. Just down the block. Come as my guest."

"I'm not much of a dancer."

"Don't worry about that," he said. "You should come anyway. She'll be there."

Righty pointed his finger across the road. How had he missed her? There at street level, her banged-up Leica aimed at the procession, was Willa. She was wearing a tank top and shorts and her hair was pulled up on her head.

His heart lurched with a sense of inevitability he couldn't quite grasp. It was incomprehensible, but he felt as if he'd known her for a long time and that he always would.

"Better hurry," Willa said. "We're going to be late."

Rose looked up from the old Singer sewing machine. She was surrounded by yards of luscious fabric and a flurry of Butterick patterns.

"You can't wait to see him, can you?"

"Who?"

"You're not fooling anyone," Rose said. "Never seen you worry about a neckline before—"

"Don't know what you're talking about." Willa emptied the wine bottle from the kitchen table into her glass. "Now hurry up."

Rose hit the speed control pedal on the Singer and pulled the hem through the presser foot. The machine had zigged and zagged through untold miles of chiffon and silk, satin and crepe, taffeta and gabardine. It had stitched dresses and gowns for every prom, dance, and special occasion in Nuckolls County over three generations.

Now Rose ran it once more, pushing fine silk over the needle plate. She would have finished the hem by hand, but there was no time. Willa hovered nearby, holding her gown up to the mirror. It was a long way from the days of flat chests, corrective shoes, and ugly dresses. They had started sewing together way back in Home Ec. Willa was always impulsive, ripping up the tissue patterns, ignoring the darts, improvising. Rose was patient, steady, careful with her pinning, working her way through the instructions, never faltering.

"Truth or dare," Rose said, mischief in her eyes.

"How old are you?" Willa asked.

"Don't be such a square. Come on, truth or dare?"

"Truth," Willa said with a huff. She took a gulp of wine.

"Which would be better?" Rose asked. "Going to bed with J.J.? Or waking up with him?"

"Don't be crazy!"

"Relax. It's just a game." Rose leaned closer to the bobbin to inspect the stitch. "I think I'm a morning person. Even with Bad Bob, I loved waking up next to him, opening my eyes, seeing his ragged face." She looked up from her sewing. "Lying there next to him always felt so inno-cent, no matter how rotten we were doing. A whole new day was ahead of us. Anything was possible. Made me feel hopeful."

"Guess I'm a night person," Willa said. "The day's done. You take a long look at your man, close your eyes, and you know you're together. Doesn't matter what's hap-pening outside in the world. For that moment, as you drift off, you know you're safe."

Rose smiled. "If Bob had been around more at night, maybe I'd feel the same."

"You deserve great love," Willa said.

"You too." Rose released the presser foot and pulled the gown away from the machine. No time to waste, she bit the thread with her teeth. "There. All done."

In a jumble of stockings and slips, they threw on their dresses. Willa helped Rose with her makeup. Rose helped Willa with her hair. Then they ran barefoot, high heels in hand, down the street to the summer dance.

The Elks was an easy stroll from the motel. J.J. entered from the quiet street into a mash of loud country music and rowdy conversation. This time he picked her out of the crowd in an instant. She was in the center of the long and narrow room, surrounded by a hundred people dancing on the slick wood floor.

She wore pale, luminous pink, a dress with a low-cut neckline that hugged her tight at the waist, then billowed out in weightless layers of fabric swirling around her thighs. He hated to take his eyes from her but he had no choice. She was not alone. She spun in the arms of a tall young farmer he'd seen drinking at Jughead's. The lucky guy had a full head of thick black hair and was built like a Chippendale's dancer. She was smiling into his face as he twirled her around the room. J.J. knew it shouldn't bother him, but the sight of her—Willa—just plain hurt.

He pushed through the mob, found the bar, and ordered an Asphalt, his father's favorite drink. The bartender had never made one but was eager to please and took instructions well. Brandy and Coca-Cola over ice with lemon. J.J. guzzled the syrupy drink, ordered another, and watched the dance from the sidelines. There were two bands: a local group named Free Beer and Chicken played decent Elvis. Then the Chuck Bauer Band took over, just two musicians, but they launched into a lilting rendition of the Tennessee Waltz.

Meg Nutting from the motel scurried over and tapped his shoulder. "Dance with me, Mr. Smith?"

"Okay, sure," he said. "I'll try."

He'd forgotten how to waltz but made a good show of it, following Meg who was well in control. He felt another tap on his shoulder. Someone was cutting in.

"Can I take your picture?" said Hilda Crispin, author of *The New York Times* best-selling *Jumbo Jet Cookbook*. A flash went off in his face.

Shrimp appeared at his side with a tall and substantial brunette almost twice his size. "My wife, Dot, wants your autograph."

J.J. smiled. "You two make quite a pair."

"She's my high school sweetheart," Shrimp said, looking up into Dot's eyes. "My shade in the summer and warmth in the winter."

J.J. autographed a napkin just as Righty Plowden and a frizzy blond woman danced by.

"Nice night for a party," Righty said, slowing to a stop. "This is the fella I've been telling you about. Meet my bride, Sally."

"You didn't tell me Sally was such a beauty," J.J. said.

"Yup, she cleans up good," Righty said with a laugh. "Easier to bring her along than kiss her good-bye." Sally slapped Righty's bottom.

"Forty years of marriage," she said.

"Just like a hot shower," Righty said. "After a while, it's not so hot."

"You old salt lick." She poked him in the side. "Didn't know you ever took a shower!" Then the two spun off onto the dance floor as the band played "I Get a Kick Out of You."

Forty years of marriage. Not bad at all. J.J. looked across the dance floor and saw Wally surrounded by fans. Nearby, Otto told a story that made everyone laugh. J.J. searched the room for Willa. He saw Rose in a gorgeous red gown, twirling on the dance floor.

Had Willa already left with Mr. Chippendale's? Why had he even bothered to come? He was stag at the Elks. Enough was enough. He'd done his public relations duty, and now it was time to leave.

He slugged down one last Asphalt, his third, and made his way toward the bright green exit sign wavering at the end of the hall. He had wedged his way into a group of people blocking his path when he heard a voice calling him.

"You leaving?"

He was pressed on both sides by farmers and wives. He turned and came face to face with Willa.

"Uh. Hi," he said. "Big day tomorrow. Gonna go get some rest."

"Mmmm. I understand, but I don't see how you can leave without asking me to dance."

His arms were full of her, his nose inches from her luxuriant hair. The band played Frank Sinatra's "The Nearness of You."

> It's not the pale moon that excites me,
> that thrills and delights me, oh no . . .
> it's just the nearness of you.

She was a better dancer than he, but she made his clumsy footwork seem smooth. If only his head wasn't spinning. How much brandy did that infant bartender put in his drinks?

"Sorry about running off yesterday at the water tower," Willa said. "You did a wonderful thing, yesterday, saving my stupid brother."

"Uh-huh. He's a nice kid."

Willa gave him a squeeze. "Thanks."

"'Welcome," J.J. said. He remembered to breathe as the band played . . .

It isn't your sweet conversation
That brings this sensation, oh no . . .
It's just the nearness of you.

"You okay?" Willa asked, looking into his face.

"Not sure." J.J.'s mind was thick and his feet felt heavy. He searched for a world record to organize his thinking, but the facts in his head were hopelessly confused. "I can't remember if the largest country line dance was 3,770 people or if that was the biggest hula dance—"

Willa laughed. "Wow. You forgot your stats. Hold the presses."

J.J. chortled, a bit too loudly, then stepped on her toes. But she didn't seem to notice. She was singing along. . . .

When you're in my arms and I feel you so close to me
All my wildest dreams come true.
I need no soft lights to enchant me
If you'll only grant me the right
To hold you ever so tight
And to feel in the night
The nearness of you.

"Thanks," she said as the music stopped. People around them applauded, and the room began to spin ever so slowly. J.J. reached out and grabbed for Willa's arm.

"I need some fresh air," he said.

• • •

The railroad tracks ran right alongside the grain elevator, twin towers in the night, just a block or so from the Elks. Moonlight glinted off the rails and down the tracks. A ground fog was pushing in.

Willa held J.J. by the arm, steadying him as they walked away from the sound of the dance hall and into the silence of the country. She sure liked this J.J, and she actually felt lighthearted. But she had to be careful. If she didn't protect her heart, no one else would.

She stopped, took off her heels, and wiggled her toes. "There, that's better."

"Was that your boyfriend you were dancing with?" J.J. blurted.

Willa chuckled. "I used to baby-sit Barney. He's my pressman." She paused. "Don't have a boyfriend."

She checked his expression. He seemed relieved. And then his brow furrowed, and he looked as if he was going to ask her The Question.

"How come no man has dragged you off to the altar?" he said.

Bingo.

"Oh, I've had offers," she said.

"I'll bet. So, why no takers?"

"Holy moley. Ask me something easy."

"Sorry. The kid put a quart of brandy in my—"

"It's okay," she said. "I was engaged once. Chet was the son of the town banker. Supposedly we were perfect for each other. Problem was, he wanted me to be just like his mom, and I wasn't about to give up the paper and stay home for the rest of my life."

"So you dumped him."

"No, he dumped me," Willa said. "But that was awhile ago. Don't think much about getting married anymore. I'm too old and too difficult for most guys."

"You're not difficult," J.J. said. "You're—you're wonderful." He leaned toward her, but she swerved away.

"Hey, cowboy. Stay in your saddle."

J.J. tried to right himself. He laughed. "Uh-oh. Maybe you'd better point me toward the Motel. I'll behave better tomorrow."

"It's just a few blocks," Willa said. "I'll walk you."

Through his own fog, J.J. recognized they were on Bloom Street. Cars zipped by and honked.

"What about you?" she asked. "How come there's no Mrs. J.J.?"

He tried, unsuccessfully, to silence a burp. "Sorry," he said. "I was engaged too. Emily told me I didn't know anything about love. She was right."

"Oh. You mean you didn't have that special feeling for her?"

"Special feeling?"

"You know. That feeling. The one that screams out: 'This is it. This is the person I'm supposed to spend my life with'."

"Aw, that feeling doesn't mean anything, Willa. I've done a lot of research on this subject—"

Willa turned her eyes up to him. J.J. found himself

staring at her; soaking up the angles of her face so he would remember. He was surprised when she said, "You've done a lot of research?"

For a moment, he was in freefall. He forgot entirely what they were talking about.

"The sensation comes down to three things . . ." she prompted.

"Oh," he said. "Symmetry, scent, and sound. The way a person looks, the way they smell, the sound of their voice. That's what love is. That special feeling is just nature's way of telling you to mix your genes. As for true love, friendship, or even compal . . . compab . . ."

"Compatibility?'

"Compatibility," he said. "I don't believe in any of that—"

"Well, I beg to differ."

She walked a few steps ahead then turned toward him.

"My mom was a nurse at the VA hospital during the war. She had a collection of Big Band records she brought to the day room to share with her patients. One night the best records disappeared, but she knew the culprit because she heard music coming down the hall. . . ."

J.J. didn't quite follow, but he didn't care. He liked the way she sounded, the way her voice played up and down the register. This beautiful woman with her asymmetrical face just lit up the night. She could have been an angel with a heavenly glow.

"You listening, J.J.?"

"Absolutely," he said.

"Well, Mom went off to confront the young vet in his room. She knocked on his door, threw it open, took one look into his amber eyes and instantly forgot why she was there." Willa laughed, remembering.

"All mom heard was Sammy Kaye's Orchestra playing on the phonograph," she said.

"Playing what?" J.J. asked.

Willa took his arm. "Oh, a sweet old Gershwin song."

"Tell me," he said.

She began to sing softly:

Love walked right in and drove the shadows away.
Love walked right in and brought my sunniest day.
One magic moment and my heart seemed to know
That love said "hello" thought not a word was spoken.

One look and I forgot the gloom of the past.
One look and I had found my future at last.
One look and I had found a world completely new
When love walked in with you.

"When love walked in with you," J.J. murmured, standing transfixed at the door of the Victorian Inn as Willa's sweet voice stilled. The terror he felt before was magnified now. She had been so vulnerable singing that song. Now he wanted to sweep her into his arms, devour her. And then what? What would he do with her?

"That was beautiful," J.J. said. "What a voice."

"What a song." She smiled up at him. "My folks have been married 35 years. They're still so in love, they had Blake when I moved away to college."

Another couple passed them and entered the motel. He saw Meg Nutting watching through the window. In a moment he'd have to say good night. He didn't want the evening to end.

"You're not convinced." ·

He smiled.

"Come to dinner at my parents' house. I want you to see true love for yourself."

"Sure," he said.

"Tomorrow night?"

"Fine."

"Good," she said. "That white Victorian with the windmill I showed you. On the edge of town. Seven o'clock."

"Okay."

She started walking away. "See you tomorrow," she called back. "Good night."

He stood outside the motel watching Willa until the fog closed around her and he was alone, again.

CHAPTER 15

"You'd think the King of Siam was coming over," her father said from the porch. "Never seen you work this hard in the kitchen."

"Come on, Dad. He deserves a nice meal, doesn't he?"

"Okay, what about your makeup?" her father said.

"Dad, stop."

"Just fooling," he said, and she could hear him chuckling to himself.

Willa checked the dinner table. She fussed over the flowers in the vase. Everything looked right. The white damask cloth and the matching napkins. Her mom's best silverware and dishes. The finest meal they could cook: rump roast with brown gravy, mashed potatoes, roasting ears, homemade rolls, and a chocolate meringue cream pie.

She went to the living room. The walls were lined with rows of books. Her father's collection, and his father's too. There were newspapers stacked on the floor, magazines piled on the coffee table. Every corner of the house looked like the reading room of a college library. Well, J.J. would see her family as they really are.

She went to the pantry, fixed her father a drink, Wild Turkey and water, then brought it to him with some crackers and cheese.

"You be good," she said.

"Don't worry about me," he said, lighting his pipe.

Actually, she was worried about everything. How she looked. How she would behave. Whether J.J. would find his way to the house. Would they have anything to talk about? Would he like her folks? Would he see what they had built, day by day, over 35 years?

She went back into the house, let the porch door close behind her. She poured herself a glass of white wine. A special bottle she brought back from Kansas City a few years ago. She went to the oven to check the pie. Then she heard clattering on the porch floorboards. Heard her dad say "Evening."

Then J.J.'s baritone: "Good evening to you, sir."

"I'm Early Wyatt. Thanks for what you did for Blake. We're in your debt."

"He's quite a kid. We'll find a safer record for him to break."

Willa washed her hands, wiped them dry on a dish towel, ran her palms over her wild hair, and went to the door. Her father and mother stood arm in arm on the porch, smiling at the guest of honor.

There he stood holding a ragged bunch of black-eyed Susans and meadow rue that he must have picked in a field. His hair was wet and freshly combed, his shoes nicely shined. He held out the bouquet, looking every bit a schoolboy, coming to take a girl out on a date for the first time, ever.

She melted.

When his pager beeped in the middle of dinner, J.J. didn't know what to do. He needed to return the call. It was Peasley. At the same time, he didn't want to be rude.

"Who's paging you?" Blake asked. "Someone important?"

"Don't be rude," Mae said. "It's none of your business."

"Feel free to use the phone," Early said.

"No hurry," J.J. said. "It can wait. I'm having a lovely time."

A lovely time, indeed, except for the unrelenting cross-examination from Willa's father. He seemed friendly enough in his candy-striped seersucker shirt and Dockers. But J.J. knew that behind the wire-rimmed glasses and pipe smoke, Early was keeping close watch. So too was young Blake, who trailed J.J. around the house, step for step.

Dinner had started off with Willa's report on *The Express*. Thanks to all the excitement over the 747, billings and collections were on target for a record-breaking month. Early was clearly tickled and raised a glass of wine to the honored guest.

Then, his opening question, an easy one: "First time to Nebraska?" Quickly he moved to more obscure and difficult terrain: "You a Ford man or a Chevy man?" A real stumper. J.J. knew it was loaded with judgment, like asking if you're a Republican or a Democrat. He looked to Willa for a clue to the right answer, but she popped up to get more food. Mercifully, the beat-up old newspaper truck flashed in his mind. He went with Ford. What a relief when Early banged the table in hearty agreement.

Despite the automotive common ground, J.J. figured Early had already decided the friendship with his daughter would probably lead to trouble. Either the outsider would take his cherished daughter away from Superior, or he'd break her heart.

Only his wife, Mae, seemed genuinely open and accepting. Maybe it was because in her eyes, lips, and pulled-up hair, he saw traces of Willa's features and a graceful map of how she would grow old.

"How's the roast?" Mae asked. "You have enough of everything?"

"Sure do, thanks. I'm stuffed. You know," he said, winding up for another story, "reminds me of a trip to Egypt last year. Measured the world's largest delicacy. It's a Bedouin wedding dish. A whole roasted camel stuffed with eggs, fish, chickens, and a sheep."

"Ewwww," Blake said. "Did you eat any?"

"No. Just verified it." It was J.J.'s third tale in half an hour. He was definitely overcompensating, a filibuster to avoid Early's questions. He wanted them to like him. He wanted them to trust him.

"Dad," Willa said, "more potatoes?"

Then J.J.'s pager went off again. Peasley summoned.

"It must be someone important," Blake said.

"Need the telephone?" Mae asked. "We're between courses. We'll bring in dessert and coffee in a few minutes."

"Here." Willa reached for the portable. "It'll be more private out on the porch."

J.J. excused himself and went outside. The night air was surprisingly cool. A great thunderhead gathered strength on the horizon. He punched in his calling card number, and Peasley answered on the first ring.

"What took you so long?" he began, his voice pinched.

"I'm at dinner, sir, and I—"

"It's over," Peasley interrupted. "There will be no record."

"What are you talking about?"

"No record," he said. "Headquarters has rejected the 747 attempt."

"That's impossible."

"The decision is final," Peasley said. J.J. could feel the sneer. "The directors made their ruling. The risks are too great."

"But—"

"You're too close to it," Peasley said. "You've lost perspective. It's time to pull out. I need you in Greece by Monday. There's another record—"

"You said you would fight for this," J.J. said

"It's out of my hands."

"But what about all these people? You can't—"

"Win some, lose some," Peasley said. And he hung up.

J.J. sat down with a thud on the porch steps.

He stared out at the puffy clouds rising in the west and the vast expanse of sunflowers before him. Ten-footers. Not even close to the world record, 25 feet 5½ inches, but they were gorgeous, saluting the setting sun, row after row, as far as he could see.

He wanted to run for the fields, disappear into all those flowers. What on earth was he going to do now? How would he ever make this right?

"J.J.?" Mae called through the screen door. "Everything okay?"

"Absolutely," he said, getting up from the steps. "Just tying my laces." He went back into the house and sat down at the table.

"What's wrong?" Willa asked.

"Nothing." What could he possibly tell her? He had promised her everything, and now it was gone.

"You sure?" she said.

"Yeah, everything's fine."

"So," Blake said. "What's your favorite place in the world?"

"The Taj Mahal," J.J. answered. He could find refuge in the records. This was the safest place for him, protected by his army of facts. "No question about it. The most beautiful place on earth."

He could feel Early's eyes measuring the response.

"What about you, sir?" he said. "What's your favorite place in the world?"

"Easy. Don't have to go all the way to India. I figure the best place in the world is my pasture. A field, a stream, some cottonwoods, and a whole lot of sky. No better place on earth."

"Oh, Dad," Willa said. "You sound like an old blister. J.J.'s been all over the world."

"I proposed to your mother in that pasture," Early said. "We were married there. Some day that's where we'll rest in peace, together forever."

He took his wife's hand. "No better place on earth, no matter what anyone says."

"Love you 65," Mae said, leaning over to kiss him on the cheek.

"65," he said, looking into her eyes.

It was their code. Those simple words and the number 65 seemed to transport Early and Mae to some faraway place. Or perhaps the phrase made the world around them fade away for just a moment, leaving them alone at the dinner table, 35 years together, and still with that spark, that feeling.

J.J. thought he heard the growl of thunder in the distance, and then Willa whispered, "Come on, let's get out of here."

The truck rolled through darkness toward the west. There was a charge in the air. The clouds, fluffy earlier, now looked black and threatened rain. Willa kept to the center of the country road. A possum waddled through the head-lights.

"Was that the longest dinner in the world?" she asked.

"Nope. Not a record."

"I was kidding."

"Me too," J.J. said. "It was a great evening. Thanks for—"

"You hated it. Sorry about my dad."

"Why be sorry? That's the way dads are. He loves you."

"Loves me 65," she said.

"Was wondering what that means."

"Goes back a long way. When I was three or four, my parents came to tuck me in one night. I told them I loved them. Dad asked 'how much?' So I thought of the biggest number in the whole wide world and came up with 65. It was the highest I could count."

"It's a perfect number," he said. "You're right. Nothing bigger in the whole wide world."

They rode in silence, bumping along the country road. The sky, the horizon, and the land blurred into a great sheet of black.

"I loved my dad that much too," J.J. said after awhile. "Makes me think of going to the beach in the summer. I was terrified of the water. He would lift me up and hold me against his warm chest. The hair tickled. He smelled so good, a cross between Ivory soap and road paint. And he would carry me into Lake Erie. He was strong and safe. I forgot to be afraid. He loved me 65."

Willa let his words trail off as the old radio played a George Strait song, "We Really Shouldn't Be Doing This." She listened as J.J. hummed to himself, miserably off key, and yet oddly in tune. She was charmed by this man. So sweet at dinner, so patient under the interrogation. Heck, he was even domesticated too. On the way out of the house, he actually helped clear the dishes. And, best of all, he had a big heart hiding under all those world records.

Why had she resisted him? Why was she so scared? What an old woman she could be.

"Where we going?" he said.

"Someplace I want to show you. It's just a few minutes from here. The sky's about to open up. Look." A crooked finger of electricity jabbed a distant field. "Good one!"

She reached under the passenger seat, brushing his leg, and produced her Leica. "I like taking pictures of lightning. They're just like snowflakes. Each strike is unique—no two can ever be identical."

Willa turned off the road and drove into a field. She stopped, turned off the lights. Silence and darkness. She could hear him breathing. She knew he was trying to make out shapes.

"Where are we?" he asked.

"Forever Field. Mom and Dad's pasture."

She got out of the truck.

"Come with me," she said, and J.J. followed her into the high grass. The air was warm and electric.

"Look," she said. "There."

A fresh flash of lightning, trailed by the rumble of thunder.

"You see the land?" Willa said. "There's a stream down there in a grove of cottonwoods."

Rain began to fall, just a few droplets on their faces, but the storm was gathering force. Willa stood beside J.J.

She wanted to touch him. Wanted him to put his arms around her. She turned to face him.

"So I got one for you," she said. "Why's the Taj Mahal the most beautiful thing you've ever seen?"

She could see him looking at her. She wondered if he thought she was beautiful too. He had known women all over the world. Why would he want a country girl from nowheresville?

"It's a perfect example of Mogul architecture," he was saying. "Sits on the banks of the Yamuna River. Almost looks like it's floating in the air."

"Tell me more."

"Took 20,000 workers 22 years to build. More than 1,000 elephants hauled the marble and precious stones."

Lightning cracked, lit up the whole sky. The storm was moving fast.

The fine hair on her arms stood up. The air was charging for another strike. She was aware of the beat of her heart.

"I knew the guy with the record for most lightning hits," he said. "Old park ranger named Roy Sullivan. First time he got hit was 1942. Only lost his big toenail. A strike in '69 got his eyebrows and loosened a screw in his head 'cause he started walking through storms with a golf club over his head—"

"Come on!" She laughed.

"Burned his shoulder in '70. Set his hair on fire in '72 and again in '73. Injured his ankle in '76 and burned one-third of his body in '77."

"That's crazy," she said.

"Craziest thing of all, was that after all that, old Roy ended up dying of a broken heart. Took his own life when he was spurned by a woman."

A streak of lighting caromed across the sky. There was a look on his face she didn't understand.

"What is it?"

"Thirty million volts per bolt. Chance of getting hit is two million to one. But you never know. You can be safe one minute, then . . ."

Then she got it, what the expression on his face meant.

"You're afraid," she said, softly.

He couldn't see a thing.

The rain slashed his face, soaked through his clothes. He held Willa's hand as she led him along a winding path in the dark. He heard water drumming on metal. Branches grabbed at his face, plants slapped his legs. Lightning flashed, once, twice, again. The storm was right overhead. He followed her up a short flight of stairs and then, he was inside, water dripping around him.

"We're home," she said.

"This a trailer?" he asked.

"An old Royal Spartanette. I bought it at an auction. Let me find you a towel." She vanished into darkness. "Shoot," he heard her say. "Power's out."

J.J. flinched as something furry brushed his face. A match was struck, a candle lit. He smelled lavender in the air, incense, and tried to fathom his surroundings. He was

185

in the dining area. Saw the built-in table and banquette. A bowl of fruit. A jar of honey. Eyes stared at him from the top of the refrigerator. Meowed.

"That's Flash," Willa said, materializing right beside him. "As in News Flash. Watch out, she likes men."

"Nice kitty." J.J. couldn't find more words. His voice box felt paralyzed. He could hear Willa rooting around in a drawer. He knew the trailer was made of cambered aluminum—essentially a modified airplane fuselage—manufactured by Spartan Aircraft of Tulsa, Oklahoma in the late 1940s. He also knew exactly what happened to aluminum when hit by lightning.

"Can't find the flashlight," Willa said. "You okay?"

"Sure." Okay for a man who had never been more frightened in his life. "This place grounded?"

"Definitely," Willa said. "Lighting rods at the front and the back. Don't you worry." She brushed past him. "Want some tea to warm up?" He was aroused by her scent, vanilla and cinnamon, blending with rain, rising on humidity.

"Right." Monosyllables, all that he could muster. There were beads of water in Willa's hair and they glittered in the candlelight. Her wet dress clung to her. She shook cat food into a bowl on top of the refrigerator. When she raised her arm, her breast rose, outlined by the light of the flame. He watched her fill the kettle at a tiny sink, turn on the stove. "It's gas powered," she said.

She took two mugs from a cabinet, turned to face him.

"Chamomile?" she asked. "It's very soothing."

"Good," he said.

She came closer. They were almost touching.

"It's cramped," she said, shaking her hair, "but it's

186

cozy." He felt the spray on his face, the smell of her hair. He was mesmerized, and reached for something, anything to say. . . .

"World's biggest mobile home belongs to a sheikh in Abu Dhabi. Five stories, eight bedrooms, eight baths, two garages." Then he stopped. "What an ass I am."

Her eyes sparkled as she laughed at him. It was now or never. He reached for her. Their lips met. Mugs dropped to the floor. He fell into the kiss like a thirsty man into a well. One hand, finally running through her untamed hair, the other pulling at the small of her back. She pressed hard against him. They broke apart, deep breaths, then came back together.

"Come with me," she said.

The bedroom was half again the size of the bed covered with pillows, taking up the entire end of the trailer. A fine old quilt was draped over a rocking chair.

Willa lit candles on the built-in dresser. Outside, lightning crackled. Inside, light danced over their bodies as they undid every snap, zip, and button, and threw their clothes all over the room.

Damp, naked, they fell into her nest of a bed. They rolled and wrestled, hungrily touching, feeling. And finally they joined together, thankfully, safely tucked into the aft section of a small aluminum shell.

It was a world record. J.J. forgot to be afraid.

CHAPTER 16

Dread shook J.J. awake at dawn. Wisps of morning light snuck through cracks in the window shades. Willa's breathing was soft and slight. Her head rested on his chest. Her lips curled up like a bow.

All he could think was: What have I done?

She would hate him for the rest of her life when she found out about the record. She would know he hadn't told her the truth last night. She would never forgive him. And the rest of Superior, hell, they might even run him right out of town.

And then where would he go? Peasley would give him the ax, and then what would he do?

He had broken his rule. He never should have ended up in this trailer. There would be hell to pay. And yet . . .

And yet he had no choice. He was falling for Willa, tumbling for her, rolling, careening. She made him feel alive. If she ever forgave him, ever took him into her life, she would discover the truth. He was an ordinary man who lived through other people's dreams. And of late he was a failure at that, too. She deserved better. She belonged with a man who shattered records for her; not one who simply rolled out the measuring tape.

He would leave, quietly, without fuss.

She pushed her nose into his neck, reached her arm across his chest, and snuggled closer, breathing a sweet dream. Then she came awake in his arms and lifted her face to be kissed. Willa. The warmth of her skin, the delicious smell, the golden hair.

He ran his fingers over her lips and pushed aside all worries beyond this moment. No man on earth could resist this woman.

And so he kissed her mouth, softly, then her throat, moving slowly, inch by inch, until he reached her knees. Gently, he turned her over on her stomach and moved his lips up her legs, across the sweet dip in the small of her back, to her shoulders. He pushed aside her layers of hair and found the warm spot at the base of her neck. The fine hairs were damp and he took his time there, kissing, pushing against her. She shivered, then began to move beneath him.

She rolled over, arching her back to stretch, and put her hands up to his face. He kissed her palms and each finger all the way to the tips.

And then they folded into each other, dissolving the last distance between them, and for the longest time they were lost, again.

He snored.

A true, window-rattling snore.

It made her laugh. She was wide awake. Open. Wide open. This feeling had ambushed her. Without planning, she let this man, this stranger, into her town, her home, her bed, now her heart.

She touched one of J.J.'s feet with her own. She took his hand. Looked at his long fingers. He had touched every part of her, and now she tingled with the fingerprints of love.

He coughed.

"You awake?" she said.

He muttered something.

"I can't believe this," she said. "It's wonderful. You are wonderful."

He gave her hand a quick squeeze.

"That's just your oxytocin talking," he murmured.

"Oxy-what?"

He sat up and stretched, rubbed his eyes. "It's a hormone," he said, falling back on the pillow. "Triggers labor contractions. Causes lactation. Bonds women to their babies and to men they sleep with. Stimulates brain receptors that create emotions. We have it too, but not as—"

A rebuff.

"Okay. That's enough," she said. "Sorry I asked." She

released his hand and turned over to stare at the clock ticking on the mantel.

Through some unspoken agreement, they pretended nothing had happened when they arose. J.J. saw Willa was guarded now. He had already wounded her. That oxytocin remark. It was stupid.

She let the cat out, made a breakfast of cornflakes, fruit, and coffee. He sat in a barber's chair as she served it on a small iron table in her overgrown garden.

Twice he caught her staring at him.

"What are you thinking?" he asked.

She poked a piece of cantaloupe. "Nothing really."

She stood, returned to the trailer for coffee, topped off J.J.'s cup. She changed the subject, coloring it with cheer. She was pretending.

"I'm so jealous of all the things you've done," she said. "Always thought I'd get away from here and travel the world. That's why the trailer hitch points out toward the road."

"On a minute's notice, you can pick up and go."

"Well, it hasn't worked out that way." She cleared off the table. "But, hey, you never know. . . ."

"You never know," he repeated.

He looked around the garden, so welcoming in daylight. Tomato plants climbed up wire cages. Flash, the chubby calico, rolled in a flower bed. Birds jostled at a feeder and honeysuckle grew along a rustic fence. A handpainted sign said: "TWO HAPPY ACRES."

J.J. felt urgently compelled to leave.

He helped clear the dishes and nearly vaulted into the passenger seat in the Ford. She listened to the farm report on the radio during the short ride. No conversation was necessary. The truck puttered through town, past the windmill, toward Wally's farm.

The oxytocin gaff kept coming back to him. How could he explain that away? He wanted to tell her how much she meant to him. What to say, how to say it? He kept silent.

They drove up the dirt path into Wally's field, and he was about to say "Let's have dinner, so we can talk," when he saw her expression freeze. There, amid a throng of reporters, standing head and shoulders above the tallest, was Wally. He was coming toward them.

He looked mad.

The television masts had fallen like timber. The banners had been yanked from their moorings. Tent poles were strewn like pick-up-sticks with clumps of canvas bunched around them. Wally had watched with befuddlement as the journalists and corporate sponsors decamped, and then he saw the old green truck roll to a stop in his mashed cornfield.

Willa and J.J. were in the cab. Together. That was strange.

Wally stalked out to meet them.

J.J. rolled down the window. "Morning."

"Where's everyone going?" Wally asked.

"What do you mean?" J.J. said.

"Look around. Everyone's packing up. Pulling out."

"I really don't know," J.J. said, getting out of the truck.

"Tell the truth. What's going on?"

Finally J.J. mumbled, "There was a snag back at headquarters. Reporters come and go. They'll be back."

"What about this?" a reporter said, right behind Wally. He held up *The Omaha Herald*. A banner headline ran across the front page:

BOOK OF RECORDS TO ABSTAIN FROM 747 GLUTTONY

Wally grabbed the newspaper. He stood just inches from J.J., casting a shadow across the smaller man's face. He began to read: "'Because of concerns about liability, *The Book of Records* announced it will not recognize the 747 eating attempt. Nigel Peasley, a high ranking official with the book, urged all record seekers in the inorganic category to cease and desist.'"

The reporters closed in on J.J. and Wally.

A young correspondent waved *The Chicago Tribune*. "When did this happen? Why didn't you tell us?"

"You know why," Wally said. "He doesn't care. It's just another record to him."

Willa was standing by the truck. There were tears in her eyes.

Wally walked over to her. "What are you doing with him?" he asked. "What's going on?"

Why was she so upset? Did she care about him or the record that much?

Then he realized exactly what had happened. He understood why she looked so devastated. He turned back to J.J., stretched out a meaty arm, and grabbed his shoulder. Spun him around.

"What did you do to her?" he shouted.

J.J. didn't have time to say a word. Wally pulled back his fist and let it fly.

Bone snapped. Blood spurted. J.J. staggered back and fell down hard.

"There," said Wally. "So much for your perfect nose."

"You knew last night the record was canceled," Willa said, eviscerating J.J. with her look. She jerked the gear shift, and the truck lurched down Wally's road. She took the corner without slowing, throwing him hard against the door.

His nose throbbed.

"I wasn't sure." His voice was muffled by a thick wad of paper towels stanching the flow of blood. Every bump and turn, every rut under the wheels sent new pain radiating across his face.

"That phone call at dinner. You didn't tell me."

He could barely breathe. "I'm sorry." He measured each word, one syllable at a time. "I fought hard for the record, but there's no way to reverse the decision. It's final."

He waited a moment, then said, "Now they're sending me to Greece."

"When?"

"Today."

"You used me," she said.

"No. I didn't—"

"You broke your promise to me and the whole town."

She didn't sob, but tears fell down her cheeks. He reached out and touched her arm. She shook off his hand.

"You think I wanted it to turn out this way? I didn't know how to tell you last night. I thought I could save it—"

They were on Highway 8 just outside of town. An empty two lane road. Willa braked hard in front of the Animal Hospital, a small cinderblock building. The truck rocked on its springs. "You're here," she said.

"Willa. Please."

"Get out."

She wouldn't look at him. He opened the door and slid from the truck. Stood on asphalt and watched her screech away.

"Willa!" he called.

The truck kept going, and his heart ached even more than his battered nose.

A poster on the wall showed the respiratory ailments most commonly associated with poultry. Another gave the five critical criteria for diagnosing a bovine hernia. The examination room was big, tiled in white, with a stainless steel table in the middle.

J.J. sat on the cold surface, legs dangling over the edge. Doc Noojin wore a white coat and a stethoscope around his neck.

"If a cow's nose was broken," Doc said, "this is what I'd do to it." He put two big hands on J.J.'s face. "This would hurt the cow, so—"

With a quick, jerking movement, he wrenched the busted nose.

J.J. let out a primal scream that silenced the hospital and the kennel. Not a beast stirred.

"There," Doc Noojin said. "Cow's nose would now be reset."

Cow's nose would now be reset. . . .

J.J. dreaded how he would look when the swelling was gone. He feared the nose that once savored the exotic aroma of Bedouin camel would never work properly again. His perfect nose.

"What about painkillers?" he said.

"Well . . ." Doc scratched his beard. "A cow with a broken nose would take phenylbutazone. It comes in a big pill."

He reached into a drawer and found a bolus the size of a salami.

"Let's see, you're about one-fifth the size of a cow, if you get my drift. You do the math."

J.J. tried to follow through the haze in his head.

"Everything will be fine in a few weeks," he heard Doc say. "Although this cow we've been talking about won't win any beauty contests for a while."

J.J. looked in the mirror. He was barely recognizable. His eyes were slits encircled by black-and-blue rings.

"Thanks, Doc," J.J. said, his voice as flat as his face.

He slid off the examining table, grabbed the giant pill, and headed for the door. Every dog barked at him as he left the hospital and walked slowly back into town. Cars and trucks ignored him as they passed.

At the corner of Central and Fourth, he stopped and

touched his nose. The pain was justified, even satisfying. It was punishment for the suffering he had caused.

He heard his dad's voice. "Stick to the straight and narrow, son. Stay in your own lane." For the first time in his life, he had ignored the advice and single-handedly caused a multicar wreck. How had he managed to screw everything up so badly?

Would he ever like himself again?

It was time to leave this forsaken place where the sky was gray and the old wind blew. J.J. looked down the empty expanse of Main Street. All the flags and banners had been carried off, the souvenir stands carted away. For a moment, Superior had tasted greatness, but now everything was back to normal. Except everything was changed forever.

CHAPTER 17

Even before the rooster crowed, Wally rushed from his bed, threw on his overalls, and went straight to the barn. He didn't bother to stop and look out on his empty fields. He didn't spend a moment studying his pasture, grass all flattened where the news organizations had built their pavilions. He was glad they were gone. They only muddied what was once crystal clear. Never mind all that. No time to look back.

There was serious work to do.

He went straight to the great contraption in the barn. He spent the morning meticulously examining every part, oiling the gears, changing the belts. He had taken the machine for granted. It ground down a 747 without so much as a squirt of oil in appreciation. Now it needed care and attention.

He scrubbed grit from the gear box, washed dust from the fans. The work was cleansing. It was, in the purest sense, a labor of love. He never wanted the record in the first place. He just wanted to show Willa he would do anything for her. And that was what he would do.

As a boy, he'd gone with his father to see the Cornhuskers play football at the Memorial Stadium in Lincoln. He remembered the inscription over Gate 4, carved in stone: "Not the victory but the action; not the goal but the game; in the deed the glory."

They were fighting words. Winning words.

The record didn't matter. Only the love did.

He changed the spark plugs and filters. When he was finally done with every crank and lever, the sun was straight overhead and it was so hot, it hurt. Arf watched from the shadows of the barn as Wally marched out to the last remaining section of the 747, the vertical and horizontal stabilizers. It was all gone but the tail fin, covered with a 20-foot wooden scaffold. He climbed up with his saw and began working on the rudder and dual hydraulic actuators. It wouldn't take long to polish off the fin. If he really chowed, without interruption, he would be done. Finally.

No matter what they did to him, no matter what they thought or said about him, they would never be able to take this away.

He would eat the plane, no matter what.

• • •

He found her by the river, sitting on the mossy trunk of an old cottonwood that had toppled into the water. She heard him coming down the path.

"I wanted to see you before I left."

"How'd you find me?" she asked.

"I made Iola talk." He smiled as best he could given the wad of a bandage across his nose. "Something to be said for looking scary."

"She shouldn't have told you. There's really nothing left to say."

"Sure there is. Please, may I join you?"

Willa shrugged. He sat down on the trunk not far from her. She was still wearing the shorts and T-shirt from the morning, but she'd kicked off her shoes and was dangling her toes in the water. The stream was flat and low. Crickets buzzed, and birds quarreled in the trees. Her face was streaked from crying.

"You didn't have to come," she said. "I'll be fine. It's better if we just forget last night happened."

"I can't do that," he said. "I'm sorry about everything."

Willa raised her eyes. "Yeah, well, it was my mistake too. I thought we were falling in love."

She reached for a stone, skimmed it across the smooth stream. Then another rock.

"The record is 38 skips," he said. "Wimberley, Texas. It was quite a—"

She motioned with her hand. Stop it.

Then she said, "I looked up the Taj Mahal. You said it was the greatest place in the world because of the architecture, the symmetry, the style."

"I remember."

"That's the difference between us. You see the statistics, the surface. I see something else."

She threw another rock.

"It's love, not marble, that made the Taj Mahal," she said. "A prince loved a princess so much he built it for her as a monument when she died."

J.J. ached as he looked at Willa. She was beautiful in ways that had nothing to do with the distance between her eyes or the ratio of her waist and hips. She saw deeply where he did not. She would have led him to those places, shown him those feelings.

"You only see the statistics and the tonnage," Willa told him. "Maybe that's why you and I were never meant to be."

The breeze picked up and sent fluffs from the cottonwood trees down onto the water.

"You're right," he said. "Wally's building you the monument. He never wanted a world record, he never wanted the attention. He only wanted to show you how much he loves you.

"I ruined something pure and beautiful," he continued. "I barged in with The Book, didn't listen to him, didn't listen to you. I destroyed something truly great."

Dragonflies zipped over the grass.

Willa's voice, when she spoke, was strained. "You should go."

J.J. took one last look at her. Memorized her face, her tiger eyes, her halo of wild hair.

"I won't forget our time together," he said.

He wanted to kiss her, but she turned away, set her

gaze on a rock far downstream. As if she were erasing him, as if he had simply stopped existing. He wanted to die.

"I'm sorry," he said again.

Then he began the long, sad climb up the path and away.

She stayed by the river all afternoon. It was her sanctuary, where she had fished with her father, floated on inner tubes with her friends. Now she had to cope with this memory: J.J., his face swollen and bruised, telling her he was leaving, that he would never forget her. The words came from him as if they made perfect sense. Leaving, remembering, good-bye.

She tiptoed into the stream and watched the carp nip at the fluffs of cotton that floated on the surface. She washed her face and dried it with *The Book of Records* T-shirt that J.J. had given her.

She had fallen fast for him and with good reason. His worldliness. Something about his funny way of projecting statistics onto everything—as if all those numbers would protect him from his feelings. Something about the way he ate corn on the cob, rotating the ear like a lathe. Something about his frayed collars. The sweet way he looked when he said her name. Willa. As if he wanted to hold the word in his mouth for as long as he could.

And yet . . .

She hated him for leading her on, for breaking promises, for making Superior worse off for having known him. She should have known better than to give herself over so quickly, to open up, to care.

J.J. was right. Wally was the man building her the Taj Mahal. He was the only one who ever had. He might be the only one who ever would. And she knew just what she had to do.

CHAPTER 18

A cloud of dust rose up on the road.
Wally recognized the truck by the clanking engine even before the old green
Ford pulled up to the porch. He knew he
should offer to tune the thing up for her.
But then he saw her, his throat went dry
and he reached for his root beer. He
choked on the aluminum grounds.

Willa stepped out of the truck and
slammed the door. Her hair was loose
and wet. She wore a white blouse, a simple skirt, and sneakers.

"Hey," she said. Arf wagged his tail,
trotted down the steps and licked her
hand. "Hi, boy."

"Evening," Wally said. "Didn't expect
to see you out here again."

"Sorry. I should have called."

"No. Glad to see you." He worried why she had come, yet at the same time, whatever the reason, he was happy just to look at her, an apparition, so beautiful.

"Get you something to drink?"

"Sure," she said.

"Juice? Beer? Stabilizer?"

"A Bud would be great."

Wally went into the dark coolness of the house. He was flabbergasted. What was she doing there? Had she noticed the 747 was almost gone, not much more than a bunch of bones in the yard? He checked the mirror on the way to the kitchen. His hair was askew and he had crumbs on his chin. Not exactly the way he wanted her to see him. This was the first time she had visited, not counting the time she came to pay her respects when his parents died. He mashed his hair down and wiped his face, hoping he looked human enough, even if his face wasn't at all symmetrical.

He rinsed metal grounds out of the bottom of a glass, filled it with beer, and brought it out to the back porch. Willa was sitting on the steps, her back up against a column, legs propped up on a bag of seed.

"How you getting on?" she asked.

"Fine," he said. "Hoping for a good harvest. Fingers crossed."

She looked out at the fields. "Sure is quiet out here."

"Sure is. All those folks made so much noise, I couldn't think straight or get much sleep."

"Glad they're gone?"

"Yup. Just me and Arf again. The way we like it."

Wally took a drink, then said, "So what brings you to the country?"

Wally watched as she seemed to search for the right words. She looked at the fin of the 747 rising against blue sky. One last section of the plane. The rest, devoured, every frame and stringer, because of his insatiable love.

Finally she spoke.

"I want you to stop. I want you to quit eating the plane."

He measured her words, thought for a while, then said, "But I'm almost finished, Willa. Just a little bit more to go."

"It's over. There's not going to be any record. There's just no point."

"There is a point," he said. "I never cared about all that. You know why I'm doing this. I wanted your attention."

Willa looked him full in the eye. "You've got my attention."

He let the moment hang. "I wasn't sure you noticed."

"Of course I did. How could I miss it?"

Willa laughed and Wally guffawed a bit too loud. The wind came up and rustled the maple tree. Arf panted. A pretty harmony. Maybe it would last just a bit longer. Nothing ventured, nothing gained.

"Want to stay for dinner?" he asked. "I've got a ham."

"Love to," Willa said.

She curled up on his old sofa. Wally liked seeing her shoes lined up neatly on top of the Persian rug that belonged to his grandma and grandpa. Their pictures, old sepia photos, looked down on the beat-up lowboy. Always stern-faced and disapproving, they seemed to smile this night.

"So, what made you decide to eat the plane?" Willa asked when dinner was over and the dishes were washed.

It was night. She was in his house. Eating his food, laughing at his jokes, sprawling on his furniture. This was the most amazing evening of his life. It had been worth every fastener, bolt, and spanner.

"It's a long story," he said.

"I'm in no hurry."

Wally filled two mugs of coffee and brought one to Willa. He set his down on the coffee table cut from a slab of oak. Then he sat down beside the woman of his dreams.

"It all started with Otto," he said.

"Hornbussel?"

"He worked in the circus all his life, mostly as a clown, traveling the country. When he was home for vacation, I used to follow him around."

Arf jumped up on the couch between them and nuzzled his nose into Willa's lap.

"Remember the day I ate the thermometer?" he asked.

"Of course," she said.

"Well, when Otto heard about it, he told me stories about the great international performers who ate dangerous things."

"Like what?"

"There was a man in London who ate gravel and rocks. They called him Lithophagus. It's Greek or something for stone eater. He was famous around the world. Another guy ate iron. People came to his shows with keys, pins, nut-crackers, bolts, and he chewed them up."

"Never heard of such a thing."

"It's all in a book that I read. French guy named Dufour made his name eating burning oil, boiling tar, and acid."

"Come on."

"He finished off his act by eating the candlesticks and candles, leaving the theater in darkness."

"This is all true?"

"Yup, and then Otto helped me cut up some car keys with a pair of wire snips. I ate them. Some nails too. From that moment, I knew exactly what I wanted to do when I grew up."

"So what happened?"

"I wanted to join the circus," he said, "but Otto wouldn't let me. Told me I'd end up like him. Drunk. Poor. Alone. He said I should stay put and grow corn. Like Dad and Grand-dad before him."

"You think you made the right choice?"

"Sure," Wally said, gazing into her face. "That's why when the plane crashed in the field that night, I thought it was a godsend. A sign from up above."

He looked into her lovely eyes. "And now I know it was."

For all his size and strength, he was so gentle. They talked for hours. He was a good man, a kind man, a man who loved her. He was smart enough, and funny too. He was peeling an orange for her with a buck knife. She looked at his hands. Cracked, weathered hands. His face wasn't handsome, but it wasn't homely. He had big shoulders and a reassuring calm.

"Did I do any permanent damage when I hit J.J.?" he asked.

"You squashed his nose, but he'll live. He left town today for some unsuspecting country."

"Can't say I'm sorry."

"I don't want to talk about him." And then, unable to stop herself, she did. She began describing the first time she saw him in the office. "Figured he was just another huckster, you know?"

Wally nodded. "You were right."

"Yeah, but . . ."

She found herself describing the ways he had snuck right into her heart.

"We ended up in Righty's field. Eggs flying toward me, rolling end over end. We tried for a world record. It wasn't his idea. It was mine!

"Then Blake tried to fly to Kansas, and J.J. climbed the water tower and got him down. Pulled the little twerp out of the clouds, deposited him safe and sound on the ground."

"The least he could do," Wally said.

Willa stared off into space. She saw a flicker of lightning, then a candle inside the Spartanette. Twenty-four hours ago she thought she had found love. . . .

Wally coughed. His face was stiff. All at once, he didn't look well. She didn't want to hurt him, but all she could do was talk about J.J. She reached over, took his hand.

"You've done something beautiful for me," she said, "and I loved it. Every girl in the world wants her prince to eat a 747 for her. "I confess. It made me feel special. It's selfish, but every time I heard the grinding noise, I knew you cared."

There were tears in her eyes.

"I never should have let you do all this. I should have stopped you a long time ago."

"But I love you."

She moved closer to him.

"If you love me, then you'll stop," she said. "You'll know I don't love you in the same way."

"What if you gave me a chance?"

"The right person has to build you the Taj Mahal," she said.

"The Taj Mahal?" he repeated, befuddled.

"What you've done for me is breathtaking. But it isn't right. And it never will be."

She could feel his pulse beating hard as she held his hand. "I'm sorry," she said.

"I know," he said. "I'm sorry too." His voice wavered.

She put her arms around him and hugged him. She felt his strength, his power, and then his body shivering. He held her like he'd never let go.

It was well past 2 A.M. The minutes blinked by on the read-out of the VCR. He sat still on the couch. After their long talk, Willa had wanted to leave but was too tired to drive. She had dozed off, her head nodding over onto his shoulder. Arf waited at the door. He had wanted to go outside for more than an hour, but Wally wouldn't move for fear he'd wake her up.

He had dreamed of this moment, Willa asleep in his home. He ran his whole imaginary life with her through his mind. Trying to understand what she told him, trying to understand where he got things wrong.

He wasn't mistaken about her. She was every bit as wonderful as he had thought since that magical day she jumped down from her dad's pickup in her blue party dress. She hadn't loved him, but he always believed she would if she got to know him. If only he could prove the strength and depth of his devotion, she would catch fire just a little. Then it would build and build, until she felt for him what he felt for her.

Now, he faced the truth. His living light loved someone else.

He thought she wouldn't mind if he touched her hair, so he caressed the curls with the side of his hand. The ringlets were soft, just like the rest of her, and that made big tears spill down his cheeks. He wiped them away quickly, afraid they would fall and wake her up. Sadness invaded him. She was in his home, on his couch, asleep on his shoulder, the culmination of his dream. But she would never belong to him.

He hadn't wept since his tenth birthday in City Park. She was the reason back then that he had stopped. Now, in some strange way, it made sense that she was the reason he began to cry again.

CHAPTER 19

Dead ahead, the island of Folegandros jutted from the waters of the Aegean. From the time of Troy, the jagged rock had been a forsaken place of banishment and exile. Sea spray brushed his face with a fine salty mist, and gulls wheeled overhead. Dripping with gloom, J.J. slouched over the rail of the wooden ferry.

A shipload of tourists in high holiday spirits cavorted around him. But he was alone, miserable, marooned. He might as well have been sailing to Tristan da Cunha in the South Atlantic, the remotest inhabited island on earth.

With unintelligible shouts from the captain and crew, the boat glided and bumped into the dock, and the passengers unloaded. The little port of Karavostassis lay a good three miles from the hotel. The steep and narrow footpaths were unfit for cars, so J.J. began the uphill walk in the hot sun. Children ran past him laughing. An American boy pointed, shouting "Mama, what's wrong with that man's nose?"

"Calvin, don't be rude," the woman said. "Sorry about that."

"It's all right," he said.

His bruised face was tinted all colors of the Mediterranean sunset. Of course children would gawk. Roasting in his blue blazer with the gilded crest, he knew he was dressed preposterously for the glaring heat. He trudged along, past the small whitewashed houses, brightened by geraniums in window boxes and bougainvillea cascading from wooden balconies. He followed the sharp twists of the stony streets until he came to the oldest part of the town of Hora, and there, the Castro Hotel.

A Venetian castle built atop a cliff to safeguard it from pirates, the Castro was the finest establishment on the island. At the noble doorway, the proprietor, Despo Danassi, welcomed her honored guest. A beautiful lunch awaited him—her specialty, *Matsata*, fresh pasta with rabbit.

"*Po po, zestee poo kanee,*" she said. Whew, it's hot. She showed him to her finest room. There was no air conditioning, no television, just the magnificent view from the balcony that dangled 984 feet above the sea.

He stared at the vast blue waters and scarcely noticed his lunch. It had been a long trip, straight shots from Superior to Omaha, New York, and Athens, then Piraeus for the ferry. A week in this tiny fishing village would do him some good. No news from the outside world. A perfect place and time to get his mind off Willa. He was a master at turning off the memories, shutting down the feelings, especially with a good distraction at hand. And there was nothing so distracting as a record attempt.

J.J. unpacked, gingerly washed his face, and changed his clothes. Then he made his way downstairs. Despo gave him directions to the taverna, and he set out into the street. A pack of children shouted excitedly. They were lined up with their yo-yos ready to go.

He tried to hurry past, but they surrounded him, tugging at his blue blazer.

"Look," one said. "World record. Yo-yo!"

Kids were the same all over the world. He painfully pulled a smile, waved, but spared them the truth. They had no chance. Fast Eddy McDonald of Toronto had a lock on the world record with 21,663 yo-yo loops in three hours.

His entourage swelling, J.J. found his way to the main square and the Taverna Nikolaos, where the world record attempt would take place. It was a simple restaurant with grape vines scrambling over an arbor at the entry. All 200 citizens of Hora had turned out for the momentous occasion. Villagers, young and old, clustered around him in awe. The esteemed man from New York. The Keeper of the Records.

J.J. was pleased to see a solid straight-back chair in front of the table that had been set out for him. The room, otherwise, had been cleared of furniture. The crowd sat on the floor ten deep around the perimeter of the room. He opened his rule book and accepted a bottle of water and a plate of figs.

In the empty space in the middle of the room, Mitros

Papadapolous, the record seeker, performed deep knee bends and jumping jacks. His eyes were dark and piercing, his mustache prodigious, and he wore a skimpy Adidas tank top and pair of shorts over his sinewy frame. Thick sweatbands adorned his head and wrists. The man was clearly prepared for struggle.

"Are you ready?" J.J. asked.

"Yes," Mitros said, "I am ready."

J.J. stood to address the crowd, assisted by a shapely young translator. "The world record in this category is 18 hours, 5 minutes and 50 seconds. It is held by Radhey Shyam Prajapati of India."

Then he turned to Mitros and held up his stopwatch.

"*Kalee epeeteekheea*," J.J. said. Good luck. "On your mark, get set . . ."

Mitros took a deep breath, then carefully aligned his head, shoulders, arms and legs.

"Go!"

J.J. punched the chronometer.

And Mitros stood absolutely, positively still.

This time Shrimp was ready for the onslaught. He might have been a few pounds short in his uniform, but he was no pushover. He knew the moment the news about Wally hit the wires, the television trucks would come charging back into Superior. What a bunch of coyotes. They packed up and pulled out when there was no record, but now they were back for the kill.

216

Shrimp beat them to the hospital. He had the barricades up and ready in the parking lot. He posted his men at the doors of the West Wing and ICU. With his own two hands, he evicted a cute St. Louis reporter decked out like an orderly who tried to sneak inside.

Wally trusted only Doc Noojin, so Shrimp called and invited him to drop by Room 239. They stood together at Wally's bedside, aghast at the tangle of tubes and flashing monitors attached to their friend. Even the branches of the great oak just outside the window seemed to reach out for Wally, as if to help.

Doc sadly shook his head. "Wasn't any warning. No idea how it happened." He wiped his eyes. "When an animal gets this way, well, you know what we have to do."

The morning press conference was just as bleak. On the front steps of the hospital, facing the wall of cameras, Burl Grimes wore his most funereal face. The news was not good, he told the nation. Wally was unconscious. Vital signs weak. He hoped the specialists choppering in from Omaha would turn things around.

"Is it food poisoning again?" a reporter asked.

"I wish," Burl said. "The situation is critical. I hope everyone will pray for Wally. He needs God's help now."

By noon, silver ribbons had appeared all over town, wrapped around tree trunks, tied to radio antennas, and pinned to the lapels of the good people of Superior. By nightfall, folks across Nebraska wore silver ribbons for Wally.

•   •   •

Room 239 was quiet except for the beeping of the heart monitor.

Rose sat on the edge of Wally's bed. A big bunch of balloons bumped against the ceiling. There were blossoms everywhere, fancy bouquets like the last time around. Now, instead of celebrating a world record attempt, the flowers seemed to decorate a tomb.

She made notes on his chart, then put it back on the hook at the foot of the bed. Wally looked so peaceful, a sleeping giant. She gently pushed the hair from his eyes and ran her finger along the scar on his shoulder from Cupid's arrow, his self-inflicted wound. She took hold of his hand, a hand she had wanted to hold all her life. It was a farmer's hand, a good man's hand. She studied his calluses, battered nails, and the lines and markings from years of hard work.

She stroked it for a while, then kissed it softly. She leaned closer to him, her nose against his neck, and smelled him. Soap, earth, flesh. She had never been this close before, or this far away.

She wiped her eyes and put his hand on top of the bedcovers, straightened the blanket, did her best to make him comfortable. She whispered, "Please fight, Wally. Please, open your eyes and live."

She kissed his scruffy cheek.

"Please don't leave me," she said. "Please get better."

She heard footsteps coming down the hall and she stood up quickly. The door swung open. The lead doctor was a 50-year-old woman with frizzy black hair and purple-frame glasses. Behind her trailed the team of specialists from Omaha.

"What's the latest?" the lead doctor asked.

"Vitals are stable," Rose said. "He's not posturing. Pupils are equal and reactive."

The experts held Wally's CT scans up to the light. One listened to his heart and lungs, peeled back his eyelids, bent his arms and legs for reflexes. Another studied the blood work-up.

"No evidence of metal poisoning," a doctor said. "Liver functions are normal. It's not hepatic encephalopathy." He pondered. "Strangest darn thing I've ever seen."

"Absolutely no medical explanation," the lead doctor said. "Only God knows." She turned to Rose. "Beep me if there's any turn," she added, and they filed out of the room.

They were of no use. They didn't have a clue. The heart monitor beeped, and Rose looked at Wally. "Only God knows," she said.

But still, she understood. She had been on duty at the hospital when the 911 call had come. She had raced in the ambulance to Wally's farm. There she had found Willa hovering over Wally, who was paralyzed on the bathroom floor.

Later, in the emergency room, she held Wally's trembling hand while he cried out that Willa didn't love him, that she had asked him to stop eating the plane.

Through the night, he wailed. . . .

J.J., that interloper, had pickpocketed Willa's heart. Instead of treasuring her, he had walked away. He had hurt her. A broken nose wasn't enough. He should suffer more. What had J.J. done to deserve her? Toss eggs? Climb a tower? What was that compared with Wally's own proofs of love?

As his fever spiked, Wally had murmured that he would try to find comfort knowing Willa was in his life as a real person now, not as a fantasy. But there was a giant hole where the dream—the love—used to be. That emptiness had sent a shudder through his massive frame, and then he closed his eyes, as if to sleep, and fell deep into a coma.

He had been gone for days. . . .

Rose tucked the covers under his scruffy chin. "Good night, my prince," she whispered. Then she went to the door and turned off the lights.

She took one last look at the big lunk in the darkness. The reason he had collapsed into a coma was simple and painful. His immunity was gone. No longer protected by his measureless love for Willa, he was vulnerable to the fatal effects of eating the 747.

At the 16 hour mark, a Corinthian column had nothing on Mitros Papadapolous. Perfectly stationary, not even sweaty, he was well on his way to shattering the world record for the longest period without moving.

The villagers, however, were bored sitting still. Against the wishes of the proprietors, a ragtag *rebetiko* band started to play. A muscular man danced the *zeibekikos*, the ancient war dance, moving in sweeping circular patterns. He slowed down next to J.J.'s table, kneeled, bit it with his teeth, then lifted it high into the air.

J.J. snatched his rule book before it fell to the ground. The dancer lowered the table, saluted, and spun off toward the other side of the room, where he balanced a glass of wine on his head. Through it all, Mitros remained unmoved and undeterred. He stood serene, like Michelangelo's David, eyes focused straight ahead.

A pretty girl with a red scarf around her abundant chest flew toward J.J. with a glass of ouzo. "Why you don't drink?"

"I'm working," he said.

"No work, drink!" she said, plopping down on his lap.

He pushed her off. "*Efharisto.* Thank you, but I'm busy."

She pouted and disappeared into the undulating crowd.

J.J. checked his stopwatch: 2 hours 27 minutes for the record. Then he looked at Mitros, the man standing still. He seemed so calm amid the whirl of dancers, so tranquil despite the pulse of tambourines.

J.J. wanted peace, too. He gazed into Mitros's strangely hypnotic eyes, and soon his mind fled Folegandros. He was back in his apartment in New York. An old woman watered a window box of plastic sunflowers, grimy imitations of the real thing. And then he was sitting on a porch under a darkening sky, watching ten foot tall, gray-striped, mammoth sunflowers turn their heads toward the sun.

Her name—Willa—ricocheted through every pathway of his cerebral cortex. Then he heard Emily's voice accusing "You don't know the first thing about love." There were flashes of lightning in the sky, and then he was struck by a bolt of understanding. For the first time he saw his own life clearly. He had traveled the world in search of something labeled greatness and had actually found it with a capital G. But because it was unquantifiable, unverifiable, he had failed to recognize it. Instead of embracing what was good and real, he had fled to the far side of the globe.

Now he sat like a man made of stone, watching another man try to make history by doing absolutely nothing. He was verifying inertia. Authenticating nothingness. All the searching, all the chasing, all the roads had brought him to this dead end? He had to wonder: Who was the real world record holder for standing still?

He came out of his trance to the loud sound of guitars and lutes, hands clapping, feet stomping and the breaking of plates and glasses. Mitros's eyes did not waver, but J.J. shook his head slowly. He had no choice. He knew exactly what to do.

He rose up from his official post at the little table. He slammed the rule book shut. Threw down his clipboard and his stopwatch. Pulled off his blue blazer and hurled it in the air. He slipped through the dancers, walked directly up to Mitros, stared into his piercing eyes, and said, "I'm sorry."

Then, without even saying *adeeo*—good-bye—he turned and raced for the door.

CHAPTER 20

Willa worshipped in the last row of the First United Methodist church.

She prayed for Wally harder than she had ever prayed in her life. Such a good man. A sweet man. An honorable man. He couldn't die now. She blamed herself for not taking his devotion seriously enough. It had been truly epic, and she hadn't seen it. How she must have hurt him. She begged God to help Wally. And she asked for forgiveness.

Never had she seen folks so worried about the same thing. Even the great flood of 1935 didn't compare, old-timers said. For days there had been a silence over the town, an eerie hush, and scarcely anyone left home. There was no carousing in the bars on Friday night, no keno at Jughead's, no bingo at the VFW.

Last night she had closed her eyes for sleep with a feeling of loathing and awakened to the same fear. She couldn't shower and dress fast enough. Even the old Ford knew this was no time to fuss and started without complaint. She turned on the radio and heard Righty Plowden's voice. He was on Country 104 to make a special appeal. The latest reports from the hospital were bleak. Wally's condition was critical and worsening. Nate Schoof and Otto Hornbussel had been summoned to his bedside at 3 A.M., and a minister was at the ready. "No one recovers from a coma this deep," Righty said solemnly. "Let's dedicate today to Wally. Let's pray for him at church, pray for him wherever you are."

Willa turned off the radio and slowed down for the traffic around the hospital. Vehicles from all over the state were lined up on the shoulder of the road, and the parking lot was jammed. Bouquets and cards for Wally covered the steps of the main entrance.

The old brick church at the corner of Fifth and Kansas was also overflowing. She spotted her parents in the last row. They had saved a space, and she wedged herself between them. Pale light in shades of red and blue streamed down from stained glass windows. It felt good and safe.

After hymns and a sermon, the congregation prayed silently. Willa thought she could feel the intensity of their petitions. She could hear the whispers of her mother's offerings to God. Someone coughed. A baby whimpered.

And then the tranquility was shattered by an amazing sound, far off, beginning faintly, haltingly, then steadily growing louder. Heads looked up from worship. People rose to their feet. Willa clutched at her mother's hand. They could not believe the noise.

The roar was clear and unmistakable—it was the snarl of Wally's grinding machine. It boomed through the church and all across Superior. But how was it possible? Wally was in a deep coma in the hospital. And yet the grating grew.

For years they had all turned away, trying to ignore this noise, but now Willa ran toward it from the church with the congregation flowing behind her. She saw friends streaming from their homes. From all directions they rushed toward the sound coming from Wally's farm.

They followed the road north out of town, past the windmill, then took the shortcut, marching across the Mullet family's fields. Arm in arm, the folks of Superior hurried to the meadow where the airplane had crashed.

There in front of Wally's barn, they saw a man standing next to the great machine. He had giant tinner snips in one hand and a chunk of airplane in the other. The expression on his bruised face was absolutely determined. This man, the outsider, was grinding down the last pieces of the 747.

He was the last soul on the planet who would ever have imagined eating sheet metal. But suddenly the whole world had looked entirely different to him.

He had traveled to Greece and back to get to this place and this moment. He knew for the first time what he wanted in life. He knew where he needed to be, though he had no idea if they would take him back, let him become a part of this special place.

The return trip to Superior reminded J.J. of another world record: the longest continuous voluntary crawl—forward progression with one knee or the other in unbroken contact with the ground. The mark was 31.5 miles set in 1992 by Peter McKinlay and John Murrie of Scotland. J.J. had traveled more than 8,000 miles on his hands and knees to come back to this town.

He saw the folks gathering in the cornfield. They watched him silently as he pushed the metal down into the teeth of the contraption. Then he took his finger off the red button and the machine stopped grinding. He cleared his throat.

"I know I let you down," he began. "I'm sorry for what I did."

He searched the crowd for Willa but could not find her. What if she hadn't come? What if she had left Superior? He wanted to explain to her more than anyone. The words kept coming . . .

"I never really understood what Wally was doing with this plane. But now I know. It was an act of unselfish love, and I hijacked it for a business opportunity."

He saw Nate Schoof, arms folded across his chest.

"I hope you'll accept my apology," J.J. said, "and forgive me for any harm."

There was hardly a murmur. Perhaps there was nothing he could say to convince them he really cared. All he could do was the one true thing he knew and felt.

"I've come back," he said, "because I want to help finish what Wally started."

He took the red bucket from its place beneath the contraption. He mixed water with the shavings and made a porridge that he stirred with Wally's wooden spoon.

"This is for Wally," he said, and then he took his first bite of the 747. The gritty goop scratched his throat on the way down, but he kept eating. Spoon after spoon. He could feel the eyes of the town on him. He didn't care what they thought. He would finish the 747 all by himself, no matter how long it took.

He would do it for Wally. And he would do it for himself.

Then he saw Nate break away from the crowd and come toward him. J.J. stood up, spoon in hand, unsure what Wally's best friend would say or do. The science teacher's face was inscrutable. Then Nate opened his arms wide to J.J. and hugged him. A good, strong hug.

"Welcome home," Nate said.

"Good to be home."

Nate walked quickly to the ladder beside the remnants of the plane's fin. He climbed up a few rungs, pulled a loose chunk from the well-picked carcass, then went to the contraption. He had watched Wally feed the beast a thousand times, and now he flipped the switch and shoved the metal down into the grinder. It had only been a week, but how he had missed that hideous roar. The machine churned and chugged and finally spit out a good bucket of grit.

With the old wooden spoon, he mixed the grindings with a can of SpaghettiOs that he found in Wally's house. Then he proceeded to clean his bowl. He knew the warnings about the health risks, had watched them pile up on his buddy's kitchen floor, but he didn't care. If love had protected Wally, now it would protect him too.

A single file of townfolk took shape and snaked across the field. Everyone wanted to eat a piece of plane. Everyone wanted to take a stand for one of their own. Shrimp stepped forward next. He hauled a hefty piece of the vertical stabilizer—six pounds, he reckoned—to the machine and jammed it into the gnashing teeth. Then, mixing the shavings with a few cans of Green Giant sweet peas, he ate every single bite. Stuffed with aluminum, he trudged to his car. The official police weigh-in was that day. The 747 would be his godsend too.

Word swept across the town. Trucks began rolling up with families toting casseroles and Tupperware filled with Sunday dinner leftovers. The line zigzagged across the pasture, past the windmill, and over two gentle hills. One by one, the proud residents of Superior filed forward to partake of a giant, spontaneous, potluck jumbo jet picnic.

Mrs. Crispin of cookbook fame set up beside the great machine. With homemade preserves from her larder—strawberry, peach, and plum—she mixed the grindings in large pots.

Meg Nutting looked doubtfully at the bowls. "Wish you had cherry," she said, and took a good-size heap of peach.

Otto Hornbussel, in his pajamas, bathrobe, and slippers, did the same. "Hope this doesn't trigger Alzheimer's," he said with a twinkle. Then he reached for J.J.'s hand. "You're Okay by me."

Righty clapped J.J. on the back. "You had us fooled pretty good," he said.

The flat-faced waitress from the Git-a-Bite smiled for what could have been the first time in her life. Cynical reporters jettisoned their detachment and joined the line.

Early and Mae Wyatt ate a few bites. Young Blake used his hands to stuff his face, and then tried to slip some of the grindings into his pockets to keep forever. J.J. stopped him. "No cheating," he said.

All day and into the evening, old and young, husband and wife, brother and sister feasted together on the last morsels of the 747, as the pictures were broadcast live to the country, in bedrooms and boardrooms, and beamed via satellite to every corner of the world.

Even in his coma, Wally heard the grinding.

It dug its way into his unconscious and woke him right up. He opened his eyes to a horrifying sight. One thousand people trampling through his field. His great machine spewing smoke. He had promised Willa he would stop eating the plane. He had sworn to her it was over. But now . . .

The picture sharpened and his eyes focused. He was in a forest of flowers and balloons. His meadow was an image on a television screen hanging above his hospital bed.

The door flew open and Rose rushed in.

"Oh, thank God," she said. "You're awake."

"What the hell's going on?" Wally asked.

"You've been in a coma for a week." We thought we had lost you."

He rubbed his eyes and scruffy face. "No, I mean what's happening at the farm?"

Rose went to his side, looked up at the screen. "They're

finishing what you started, Wally. They're showing you how much they care and how much they want you to get well."

He scratched his chin. "Can't believe it," he said. "I heard the grinding. It was like my machine was calling to me." He flipped television channels. The live images from the field were everywhere. On CNN, Michel Lotito was blubbering that no one had ever helped him eat anything before.

Then he saw Willa, the very last person in the single-file line. Everyone else had eaten a share of the plane. Now just the navigation and strobe lights were left. She picked them up, took them to the contraption, and ground them up. Then she put some strawberry jam in a bowl, stirred in the grit, and, with a big smile, ate the last bites of the airplane.

The 747 was gone.

The crowd in the field cheered.

With a swipe of his great hand, Wally brushed the tears from his cheek, then pushed the mute button on the remote. He turned to Rose, all pink and pretty, with a silver ribbon in her hair. She had her eyes fixed on him.

"I made a world-class fool of myself," he said. "I ate an airplane for a woman who doesn't love me. How many people can say that?"

"If loving someone who doesn't love you back makes you a fool, then we've got two in this room, not just one."

"Come on," Wally said. "What are you talking about?"

"Think about it. Who folds your socks, cleans your fridge, and picks ticks off Arf?"

Wally considered all the magically made pot roasts, the

ironed shirts, the neatened cupboards, and, especially, the long walks and talks over the years. "I hope I said thank you. I'd be in a heap without you. But I never thought—"

"It's okay," she said, busying herself with his pillow. Fluffed it and put it back behind his head. "I didn't want to get mushy when I knew we were just friends."

Now Wally looked at Rose with new eyes. He noticed her shiny brown hair and the sweet way she filled out her uniform. All at once, he saw someone who'd taken care of him while he'd been looking elsewhere. Someone who stood by him without asking for a thing. Rose was his dear and loyal friend and yet he hardly knew her.

"I feel like a fool all over again," he said. "I should have noticed a long time ago, but I guess there was a 747 in the way."

He reached out for her hand. "Rose, I'm sorry."

"Well. The plane's all gone," she said.

Wally had mischief in his eye. "When do you get off work?"

"Right now."

"You know what I'm going to eat for you? I saw a locomotive in the junkyard in Hastings—"

She grinned. "Whoa, not so fast, big boy. You've got some healing to do before you go eating anything for me."

Wally wiggled under his great mound of white sheets. "Please don't quit on me, Rose."

"Now, why would I do that?" She came closer to him, put her hand on his forehead. "How do you feel?"

"I've had better days," he said. "But I feel hopeful."

"That's good. Me too."

He looked up at the IV bag dripping down into his arm. "I'm hungry. When they let me out of here, can I take you to supper?"

"Sure, Wally," she said with a chuckle. "As long as it's no-fat, no-iron."

"Sounds delicious."

Then the most extraordinary thing happened. Wally grabbed Rose and, before she could protest, pulled her down. And he kissed her.

CHAPTER 21

Burl Grimes stood on a motor oil crate in the middle of the field. It was 92 degrees, and yet the hospital chairman was clad from head to toe in mortuary black. Willa felt almost faint from anxiety.

"I have another announcement," Burl said.

The crowd gathered around. A hush fell. When he was sure he had their attention, when all of the cameras were pointed, he began to speak.

"On behalf of the hospital board, I am pleased to announce that Wally is out of his coma. He's watching us on live television this very moment. Our boy is back."

The town hooted, waved, and jumped up and down. Unprepared, overcome,

They stopped at the edge of the cleft in the ground. The wind rustled the trees. Until this moment, he had never belonged anywhere. Now he wanted to stay by her forever.

He was about to speak when Blake came running across the field. "J.J.," he shouted, "phone call! A guy with an accent. Says it's urgent. Hurry!"

"Damn," said J.J.

It could only be the last person he wanted to hear from in the whole wide world.

J.J. braced himself for a lashing. He had walked out on Mitros Papadapolous in the middle of a record attempt. He had embarrassed The Book. Nigel Peasley was surely calling on some sadistic errand to can him or make him redundant, as the Brits so elegantly put it.

J.J. ran into Wally's house and picked up the cordless phone near the front door.

"What in bloody hell do you think you're doing?" Peasley began, his voice squeaking. "I told you there would be no record! Now look what you've done. It's a disaster. You've got the whole world watching again—"

"But, sir," he began. *Sir* . . . It was a reflex, to bend down before his boss and take the punishment. He felt a hand on his shoulder. It was Willa.

"I'll be getting along," she said. "You've got work to do, and I've got a paper to put on the street."

"Wait," he said. "Please wait."

"Well?" Peasley was shouting. "What's your excuse?"

J.J. walked out onto the porch with the cordless phone. He looked at Willa, then at the people of Superior standing in the field. His eyes landed on Blake. A little boy who had desperately wanted a world record, a little boy the very same age J.J. was when he decided The Book would be his life. Fourteen years, fourteen editions. From Marrakech to Zanzibar, so many adventures raced through in his mind . . . so many pogo sticks, jump ropes, dominoes.

Then the words erupted. . . .

"I quit."

Silence on the other end of the line.

"We don't want your world record," J.J. said. Then he remembered what Willa had told him at the bar: "We don't need your brand of greatness."

"Rubbish," Peasley said. "You can't quit! You've got the next edition—"

J.J. dropped the phone. It bounced down the steps and landed in the grass. He offered his arm to Willa and she accepted. He was lifted by a buoyant feeling, as if he might float. Together they started across the meadow.

With the twilight, peace returned to the Republican River Valley. And the high-pitched voice still screaming on the telephone in the grass was no match for the old wind.

They sat on the cottonwood trunk that reached out over the river. The moon was up. Their shoes were off and they dangled their feet in the water. She was tempted to take a swim. Maybe the cool water would straighten out her head.

So many questions. Why had J.J. come all the way back to Superior? Was it really to finish off what Wally had started? Or did he want more? Heck, he quit his job right in front of her. And now he was spouting words about love. What happened to this guy in Greece? Was it real or just too much ouzo? She needed to know.

"So," she said, "would you eat an airplane for someone you loved?"

"Holy moley," he said. "Ask me something easy."

Then he leaned toward her. "Sure I'd eat an airplane for you, but only if you loved me."

She didn't know whether to believe him. The willows rustled in the breeze. Sammy Kaye started singing in her head. . . .

Love walked right in and drove the shadows away.
Love walked right in and brought my sunniest day.

"This is all kind of crazy," she said at last. "I mean, we barely know each other."

"That's the whole point. It is crazy. Makes no sense at all."

"Then how can you be sure what you're feeling? How do you know?"

"I just do," he said. "I've got all the facts and formulas, but in the end, it's just a special feeling—"

She listened to his voice, and she felt herself beginning to believe again.

One magic moment and my heart seemed to know
That love said "hello" though not a word was spoken.

"I need to know what happened to you that morning in the Spartanette," she said. "Why you pulled away—"

"I was afraid."

"I scared you off?"

"No. I scared myself off."

He looked down at his blurry reflection in the water. "I'm just another John Smith from Ohio. How could I ever be worthy of you?"

She reached out and touched his rumpled shirt, tousled his messy hair. "I like you, John Smith from Ohio."

"I like you, Willa Wyatt from Nebraska."

It was a good place to begin. They had thrown eggs and chased lightning. Maybe it was time to open up for more. The night was still, except for a bullfrog honking on the banks. She threw her head back and looked up at the sky.

One look and I forgot the gloom of the past.
One look and I had found my future at last.

"Will you ever let me back in?" J.J. said into the silence.

Willa was lost in memories. A salesman with his leather-bound books. A banker's son with all the money in the world. A guy with a gilded crest on his blue blazer.

"I'm afraid, too," she said.

"Give me another shot. Where would you be if your mom hadn't given your dad a second chance?"

He slipped off the tree trunk into shallow water and turned to face her. His eyes were so blue, and even his nose seemed its fine former self. Her knees touched his waist. She saw how much he wanted her. His arms were open and waiting. She let herself go into his warmth.

239

"Let's make one perfect day," J.J. said. "And if it feels right, let's make another one tomorrow."

All her brain chemicals were firing now, and deep inside, she knew it was there, that special feeling. Sammy Kaye's voice came to her again.

One look and I had found a world completely new . . .

He leaned into her. Their lips touched. A soft, soothing kiss that caught fire. He moved his mouth over her face and neck, then plunged into her hair, and whispered words that dissolved her last resistance.

"Love walked in with you," he said.

"Yes," she said. "Love walked in with you."

AFTERWORD

It's late. The sun is setting over the fields. At any moment, Willa will return from her newspaper run. I'll hear the Ford coming up the lane, rattling the way old junks around here do.

I live in the middle of nowhere now, or the middle of everywhere. All depends on how you look at the map. This is where I belong, and I count my blessings that after wandering the world, I finally found my place.

As I write, I sit in a little wood workshed, just a few yards from an old aluminum Spartanette. The fading light touches the photographs on my wall. I prize three pictures above all the rest.

The first is of my friend Mitros

Papadapolous. He actually stood still for almost two days without realizing I had left the island of Folegandros. He shattered the world record, earned his place in history, and was kind enough to send me a fine bottle of ouzo when he heard my news.

That leads me to the second photo on my wall. It was taken in front of the Taj Mahal the day I asked Willa to be my wife. Look closely in the background, and you'll see some old friends. One balances on a single leg while the other waves the world's longest fingernails.

The third photograph is from a farmer's field. It shows 1,104 people standing next to a red barn and a great gash in the ground, measuring 231 feet 10 inches, the exact length of a 747. These people—friends and neighbors—finished the work of one good man who set out to eat a jumbo jet. It took them 7 hours and 47 minutes, every second televised to a global audience of more than one billion people. And I can say with absolute authority that no official world records were broken.

No official world records were broken. . . .

Of course, the truth is different. You see, so many records were broken that summer in Superior, the kind that really count, the kind that never end up in books, newspapers, or on television. A man helped his best buddy build a magic contraption so he could eat an airplane. A woman never left the bedside of a friend in a coma. A boy wanted his sister to find happiness, so he brought the world to her door.

At first, I didn't recognize the majesty in these moments, but then in this age where bigger is always better, people rarely do. That, I think, is the challenge. To

242

know true greatness when we see it. To appreciate it when we have it. To embrace it while it lasts.

And that's exactly what Wally and Rose have done since that day in the hospital when he awoke from his slumber. The two have barely let go of each other and live in rich contentment on the farm. Wally is working hard on a new idea—bovine Jacuzzis. Mellow, happy cows, he insists, make healthy cows. So he and Nate Schoof are busy building a prototype in the barn.

Now to the outrageous proposition that began this book: *This is the story of the greatest love, ever.* You may counter with Romeo and Juliet, Antony and Cleopatra, or perhaps even your own personal story. And that is precisely my point. Each one of us—even mere mortals named John Smith—can claim the record for the greatest love, ever, if we can only cast off our ambivalence and recognize it when we find it, pure and true.

I keep a scrap of paper pinned to my bulletin board, even though I've long since memorized the words from the Japanese poem:

I have always known
That at last I would
Take this road, but yesterday
I did not know that it would be today.

My old road ended here in Superior, and I have ventured forth on a new path. I've begun compiling a brand-new book of records. It's not what you'd expect—God knows I'll never beat Peasley at his game—but I don't care.

I'm calling it *The Book of Wonders*, a chronicle of all

the amazing feats that go unnoticed in this world, the achievements with no entries in big books, no live shots on television, no roadside attractions. I know an old woman in New York who belongs in this book—she waters plastic sunflowers every day. It may seem crazy to some, but I know the truth. She cares.

I'm looking for stories about everyday wonders, authentic moments of greatness and splendor around the world, and I welcome your submissions. I've set up a Review Committee—you know what I mean—and I pledge to answer courteously and promptly.[1]

Perhaps someone has built the Taj Mahal for you, or even eaten an airplane. Or maybe it's something smaller but just as exalted. Maybe every night, driving up the lane, a special person just honks the horn for you. It doesn't sound like much, but listen closely . . .

The front door opens and you can hear the hurried footsteps.

[1]Kindly send your submissions to *The Book of Wonders*, P.O. Box 51, Superior, Nebraska, 68978–0051. Or e-mail your entries to recordkeeper@ thebookofwonders.com.

AUTHOR'S NOTE

I am indebted to Mark Young, former CEO and publisher of Guinness Media Inc., and his staff in Stamford, Connecticut for their guidance, information and encouragement. My thanks also go to Guinness World Records Ltd. in London. The records and many of the descriptions in this story are derived from their extraordinary books and database. The kids' letters in Chapter 2 were inspired by actual children's submissions to the record keepers. Any factual inaccuracies, of course, are my own.

I am also grateful to the various world record holders who shared their experiences, especially Michel Lotito of France, the world's greatest omnivore (8 tons of metal over 22 years) and Ashrita Furman of New York, the record holder for breaking the most world records (60 and going strong). I will always treasure the image of indomitable Ashrita one October weekend. Clutching a 10-pound brick for 30 hours 52 minutes in an uncradled downward pincers grip, he shattered the world brick-carrying record by walking 85.05 miles on a decrepit high school track in Jamaica, Queens.

To the people of Superior, Nebraska, I offer special appreciation. For their welcome, wisdom, and friendship, I am particularly grateful to Sandy and Lefty Bothwell and Beth and Chuck Fowler. Joyce, Sam, and Scott Baird generously opened their doors and many others in Superior. I was always made right at home by the morning crew at the Gas 'N Shop, the lunch crowd at the Hereford Inn, and irrepressible Russell Thomas and his gang at the grain elevator in Webber, Kansas. For local lore and answers at all hours, I am beholden to Bill Blauvelt, editor and publisher of *The Superior Express,* and his wife, Rita.

For technical information on the jumbo jet, I consulted Guy Norris and Mark Wagner's *Boeing 747: Design and Development Since 1969.* I also conferred with Glenn Farley, aviation specialist with KING-TV in Seattle, and Dan Gellert, former 747 pilot.

For the chemistry of attraction, I used many sources, including Simon Levay's *The Sexual Brain,* Deborah Blum's *Sex on the Brain,* Anthony Walsh's *The Science of Love: Understanding Love and Its Effects on Mind and Body,* and Claudia Glenn Dowling's "The Science of Love," in *Life* magazine (February 1999).

For additional material on Michel Lotito, Monsieur Mangetout, I relied on Robert Chalmer's article "Guess Who's Coming to Dinner" in *The (London) Observer* (January 1994). And for background on stone and iron eaters through the ages, Ricky Jay's *Learned Pigs & Fireproof Women* is the definitive work.